Also by Marilyn Hering
A Woman Possessed
(Book One of The Paterson Series)

A Woman BELOVED

MARILYN HERING

PROMINENT
BOOKS
EDGE

5830 E 2nd St, Ste 7000 #9983
Casper, WY 82609
USA

"Remember"

Remember me when I am gone away,
Gone far away into the silent land;
When you can no more hold me by the hand,
Nor I half turn to go yet turning stay.
Remember me when no more day by day
You tell me of the future that you plann'd:
Only remember me you understand
It will be late to counsel then or pray.
Yet if you should forget me for a while
And afterwards remember,
Do not grieve: For if the darkness and corruption leave
A vestige of the thoughts that once I had,
Better by far you should forget and smile
Than remember and be sad.

—Christina Rosetti

Absence is the highest form of presence.

—James Joyce

For Walter, always

PART I

New Beginnings

Maggie McGarrity attempted to ignore the aches, pains and the persistent cough she felt throughout her body. After all, it had only begun this morning. She could wait a few days before seeing Dr. Mary at the Women's Alliance. She studied her beautiful baby, smiling at her from the makeshift crib Sean had made. Its rough edges always caught her dress, although she didn't mind. He was a wonderful husband and she knew he loved her dearly. It wasn't his fault he was on strike more often than not. The Paterson silk mills were notorious for them. She lifted the child from the cot gently, kissed her eyes, nose, lips, held her to her breast.

"It's for you I'd better get cared for," she said, amidst the baby's smiling response which seemed an agreement.

She had told Sean if she didn't feel better soon she'd go to the Women's Alliance. When he returned from the strike line with the other dyers' helpers, he'd know where she was. Although she hated leaving her daughter Kathleen, there was little she could do. She knew Carrie, her dearest friend in the tenement, had long since left for work as a cook at the Lafferty estate.

The Alliance, as usual, bustled with activity when she arrived. Surveying the room, she saw Eleanor Lafferty, to Maggie's way of thinking a saint who walked the earth she had given so much of herself to help the poor. Mrs. Lafferty was taking a child's temperature. She was very mysterious, she was, leaving Charles Lafferty who owned a major silk mill in Paterson and returning to work at the Alliance. There wasn't a worker who didn't love her for all the care she gave them, as did Dr. Mary, who never charged if they couldn't pay. They especially admired Eleanor Lafferty who started working life in the mills, and never forgot where she came from.

Maggie finally caught Eleanor's eye since Dr. Mary was no where in sight and approached her.

"I'm feelin' poorly, Mrs. Lafferty."

"I see that, Maggie. Your face is flushed. Follow me, will you?"

She led her to a small room used for examining patients and placed her stethoscope upon Maggie's chest.

"Now breathe deep as you can and then exhale."

She did as she was told and could see a frown on Mrs. Lafferty's face, which deepened after she felt her forehead and took her temperature.

"You're burning with fever. You'll have to stay overnight."

Maggie began to button her coat, turn up her collar.

"Can't do that. There's my baby and my husband. Could I just get some syrup for the cough?"

Eleanor did not want to frighten her by describing the deep, rattling sound she heard in her lungs when she'd pressed the stethoscope to her chest, much worse than when she had treated her other times.

"I'll be fine. Really I will. I can't stay overnight. I just can't."

Eleanor sighed. Another stubborn woman risking her health to keep her family afloat at all costs.

"Let me confer with Dr. Mary."

Mary insisted she stay overnight.

She brought her to a bed, undressed her much to her protests, bathed her with alcohol to try to bring down her rampant fever, gave her a strong dose of cough syrup and medicine.

In the morning when Eleanor returned, she began her daily routine of checking the patients. She approached Maggie's bed. Her skin had darkened to an eerie mahogany color. Rattling sounds emanated from her throat. She appeared tortured as she gasped for breath.

Then nothing.

Dr. Mary had just arrived. Eleanor ran to her.

"Come quickly!"

She had never witnessed such a change in a person's appearance and condition so quickly.

They hastened to her bed. Mary took her pulse.

She was dead.

Eleanor and Mary knew immediately it was impossible this death was the result of the usual flu that struck so many of the mill workers each winter. Their suspicions were confirmed when by the end of the day fourteen more workers arrived, all with similar symptoms and within days were dead. Mary ordered Eleanor, Nora Pennington, and Brigitte O'Hara, their new nurse, to wear masks at all times. Mary suspected the enigma of such fatal deaths came from a virulent strain from the flu, and her suspicions were verified when Eleanor brought in the morning papers a few days later.

A flu epidemic. The newspaper said a soldier at Fort Dix appeared first to fall victim. He had just returned from duty in Europe. The ultimate irony was he had survived the dangers of the battlefield during the Great War and died of the flu upon his return.

Dr. Mary frowned.

"The papers say crowds are to be avoided and public funerals banned to prevent the spread of the disease. The city of Newark rented a vacant furniture warehouse to use as an emergency hospital to help handle the overflow." She looked around at their sorely inadequate facilities. "I wish we had a place like that but we'll have to make do, God help us."

Days passed. Weeks passed. The pandemic worsened. Death became so prevalent a person perfectly healthy one day was dead the next. Within three days that September the newspapers reported more than two thousand new cases throughout the state.

Dr. Belli, head physician at St. Joseph's Hospital, visited the Women's Alliance to supervise and help the best he could.

"It's common experience for me to speak with a person healthy one day and then come across him a few days later on an autopsy table," he sighed.

When Eleanor walked to her apartment she saw many people with garlic poultices around their necks. She wore one herself. Dead bodies were accumulating faster than they could be buried. At first city employees and firemen helped to dig graves. But they could not keep up with the overflow. Teams of horses had to be used to plow trenches used as mass graves. Schools closed. Eleanor, Mary, Nora, and Brigitte worked staggeringly long hours, only to find most of their efforts in vain.

Seeing people she knew from the mills that she could not possibly help began chipping at her frail sensitivity which she usually coated with armor quite well. Yet, she carried on. They deserved no less. So many died. She had to pronounce Nora who had taught her ribbon weaving when she worked at the mill dead, as was true of Florrie, who had befriended her from the first day she worked at Lafferty's Silk Mill. So many others succumbed. Within a few days.

She stared out the window to see that Paterson now looked like a ghost town with almost everyone clustered inside their homes fearing the flu contagion.

And praying.

A vehicle approached the Alliance from the direction of Silk Road. She immediately recognized her estranged husband Charles' new Pierce-Arrow and Miles, his chauffeur. But why would he stop here? She had not seen Charles, Dr. Mary's brother, since the day they had separated, having decided to try to each in their own way heal from the death of their child, not realizing how sick he was, Eleanor leaving him to run away with Dante Ravelli, the charismatic union leader who came to help the workers during the Great Silk Strike of 1913. The death of her beautiful son, Robbie, gnawed at her heart every day, but with the overwhelming work that lay ahead of her at the Alliance she at least experienced some relief from her own suffering by helping others with her constant busyness.

But Charles She had no idea if he had even begun to heal from the tragedy. The last time they spoke his pain seemed insurmountable for he blamed himself for bringing Robbie, their child, to his mill to show him off. She could not forgive him for breaking his promise not to bring Robbie to the mill. It was there he contracted diphtheria and later died. Charles was a saintly man and she hoped most likely his responsibilities running the mill with its obligations was helping him to heal.

When the chauffeur helped Charles from his vehicle, her worst fears were realized. He could hardly walk.

"What's happened?" she heard herself ask, though she knew already.

The pandemic's contagion hit him as well.

Miles helped him through the door.

"He said he wanted to come to the Alliance instead of St. Joseph's."

Dr. Mary rushed to her brother's side as well and they guided him towards a bed.

Eleanor stared at this shadow, her husband. And what did she envision when she looked upon his ravaged face? Memories Their first meeting when she foolishly mistook him for the gardener at his estate that would amazingly become her future home, his kindness at paying for a doctor who saved her mother's life when she had pneumonia, their visit to Palisades Amusement Park where she had her first real experience of knowing what happiness is, his role in bringing her mother's murderer to justice. Their marriage shattered because she was possessed to senselessness by love and passion for Dante Ravelli whose memory still lived within her. And then, worst of all, their child's death.

She took his hand, his fingers sticks covered with flesh.

Charles, you're here now. And in our hands. We'll pull you through. We will."

He stared at her, then past her, and she knew the fever had overcome him. She and Mary settled him in his bed, administered medicine, covered his bed with netting.

Mary listened for the sound of his lungs with her stethoscope. "I've heard worse. We must be hopeful."

And so, day and night they monitored him while nursing the others, amidst administering to the removal of bodies of those who succumbed, disinfecting their beds, changing bedclothes, giving medications. And waiting. The symptom, it seemed, that held the answer to who survived and who did not lay in the sound of their lungs, their intense rattle indicating they were filling with fluid, near strangling. Then their tortured look. Their faces turning gray, their skin color soon becoming dark, browner still at the cheekbones. That meant the end was near.

Miles, Charles' faithful chauffeur, visited Charles every day. One day as they walked to his bed, she noted Miles' frown.

"What is it?"

"What do you think, Mrs. Lafferty? Will he pull through?"

"We must have hope. We're doing all we can to make that happen."

Miles twirled his cap in his hands.

"Truth said, and if you don't mind me sayin' it, it's been hell for him with you gone."

"What do you mean?"

"Hell. Mrs. Lafferty, he hasn't been to his mill in ages. He runs it through Kosinski."

"But how does he spend his days then? In the garden?"

Miles pursed his lips.

"Tell me. Please."

"I wish I could tell you that, but, truth told, he—drinks most of the day away."

"No. It can't be."

"But it is. And him so thin. Won't hardly eat."

By then they had reached Charles' bed.

"Please don't tell him you told me this, Miles."

"'Course not."

Miles sat a time by Charles' bed and then left, still uncertain whether Charles would live or die.

Mary and Eleanor approached Charles' bed. He stared at them, then past them. She and Mary made him more comfortable, administered medicine, covered his bed with netting.

Mary listened to the sound of her brother's lungs with her stethoscope.

She sighed.

"I've heard worse. We must be hopeful," she repeated.

Eleanor stood above Charles' bed, realized he must have lost at least thirty pounds. How much had their separation had to do with it? More sorrow and guilt for which she must try to forgive herself. And so, along with Mary, as they hustled back and forth trying to give each and every patient their best care, her mind dwelled on Charles.

Two days passed and he had not worsened, a phenomena they had given up trying to understand concerning the way the flu reacted differently in each patient. They had attended patients who had dutifully stayed in their homes to avoid the contagion. Yet, they caught it and showed up at the Alliance, dead in a few days. Others they saw daily—the postman, the fellow who delivered their precious medical supplies and they, along with Nora and Brigitte, as well as Dr. Belli, were untouched.

On the fourth day Charles opened his eyes and smiled at her as she stood above him. To her complete surprise, she burst into tears.

"My dear," he whispered.

"Oh, Charles, I do believe the crisis may be over."

"Dear God, I hope so. I've never felt so weak and helpless in my life. I owe my recovery to you and Mary."

He smiled. "No St. Joseph's Hospital for me. I know a good thing when I see it."

"It certainly didn't hurt that you fought so hard."

"Yes. I wanted life. After all. And knowing I would see you. That made it worth it."

She blushed. "Nonsense." She reached out, held his hand, which felt like dried paper.

"Oh, Charles, I'm so glad you seem to be pulling through."

They were silent a time, holding hands in shared silence.

"I've been thinking about our relationship a great deal lately," Eleanor offered.

"What were you thinking?"

She smiled.

"Oh, about our first meeting when I mistook you for the gardener and the food you gave us that helped us during that terrible strike."

"You were so pale, and thin."

"And how you may have saved my mother's life that time she had near pneumonia. Your taking us home that icy day when we slipped and slided all over the cobblestones. And your paying the doctor's bills."

Eleanor's eyes filled with tears at the thought of her mother's tragic death.

"And your paying for the investigation that led to her murderer."

"She was worth it. Such a good woman."

He attempted to change the delicate subject.

"And how about our trip to Palisades Amusement Park?"

Eleanor perked up immediately.

"The carousel! Oh, that was wonderful. I think it was the first time I can say I was truly happy."

She frowned.

"And the dark things—Dante Ravelli. I was a fool. You know, I never heard from him again after he went to Russia."

"And the worst part. The guilt we both feel over Robbie's death." Charles turned his head towards the wall.

"I don't want to talk about that."

"We must at some time. But I don't want to wear you out now. Try to get some rest."

She kissed his cheek and left him with a smile upon his face as he fell into a peaceful slumber.

Charles realized Eleanor was thinking at least some good thoughts about him, and because of it Charles' sleep was the most peaceful he had known without the help of liquor to knock him out. He was a child again, and his mother, her hair braided down her back, was showing him how to plant roses. He jumped up and down with glee when she gave him the shovel to plant his very own first rose bush. He grew up suddenly and saw Eleanor standing beside him, holding him to her heart. He felt a sense of such tranquility in the dream, as she touched his face and smiled at him.

Later, he awoke to the sound of Mary's voice.

"Time for your medicine, dear brother."

He adored Mary but wished it had been Eleanor who awakened him.

At that moment he resolved his days of absence from the mill and drinking were over. For good. But could he rise to the occasion?

Charles seemed to improve each day and Eleanor visited him besides administering to his medical needs.

"Are you still creating your beautiful flower paintings?" Charles had admired them upon his first visit to their home, remembered the shock he tried to disguise when he saw the poverty in which they lived.

"No, I'm afraid I don't have the time for them now that I did as a younger girl."

"They were beautiful and I wish you would think about returning to painting again."

She blushed and changed the subject.

"Mary was telling me the other day you were the apple of your mother's eyes, but she loved you so she didn't mind a bit. Strange, we never talked about your childhood when we were together."

"I adored my mother. When I was five or so she introduced me to gardening and that's how I got such an interest in it I'm sure. To see seeds planted in the earth and a month or so later they had life! Why, we grew so many varieties of flowers together—daffodils, tulips, roses, oh, so many. And even vegetables—lettuce, cabbage, carrots, onions, asparagus—so many others she taught me how to grow."

"I hope you're still busy with your gardening,"—she hesitated— "even though the mill takes up so much of your time."

He changed the subject.

"How I love to look back on my childhood, those early days. And she was so beautiful. Black hair and blue eyes. Just like Mary's. She wore her hair in the loveliest chignon at the nape of her neck. Sometimes when she took it down at night she let me brush it."

"What a wonderful childhood you must have had."

"I did." He frowned. "And look at me now."

"Charles, don't think that way. You're improving."

"And I'll go back to that empty house with only Mary visiting me mostly."

She changed the subject.

"Tell me about the mill."

His face became bloodless.

"Oh—just fine. We're busier than ever."

"And you're getting out, supervising every day?"

"Of course. I have to make sure Kosinski doesn't foul up."

"What would you say if I told you I heard from a good source you hardly go to the mill at all?"

"I can't imagine where you heard that."

She knitted her brows, grasped his hand.

"Charles—the truth. If we were to, say, begin again we must be completely truthful with each other."

His face brightened.

"Begin again?"

"I've been—thinking about it."

"All right then. I haven't been to the mill. It's a long story. Your leaving, and Robbie's death. So many things. But I swear, if you come back to me, I'll go to the mill each day and get back to my old self."

"And what about the other problem—your drinking?"

"Good Lord, whoever told you about that?"

"It doesn't matter."

"Eleanor, I swear if you come back to me I'll give it up."

"I don't know how serious it is at this point, but you need to stop. Period." She crossed her arms around her chest. "I want to start with a clean slate."

"Of course. If you come back, there's no reason to think I'll continue—as I have."

"Is that a promise?"

He paused.

"Yes."

"And Robbie—"

"Please…

"At least let me clean out his room—the teddy bear, the fire engine, everything. I'll make it into a sewing room, or something or other."

"But—"

"Charles, it's a beginning. We have to start somewhere."

"But the thought of it." He rubbed his temples. "I just can't do it. I can't."

"I'll—take care of it. I have to do it for myself as well as you. Remember that."

They did not speak a time.

"All right" he conceded. "But will you do it at a time I'm not home?"

"Of course."

She trembled at the thought of it, but it was a beginning and it must be done.

She let go of his hand, which felt like a dried flower, remembered too his constant goodness to her—the rose garden he installed, his kindness to Colin, her father, his monetary contributions to the Women's Alliance, even though they were separated, his adoration of his child and the wonderful father he had been until that fatal day he took him to the mill where he caught diphtheria…

"You've got to get some rest. We'll talk more as you regain your strength."

A few days later, after much thought, Eleanor approached Charles' bed. He was improving with each day.

She finally felt it was time to talk about the more serious aspects of their reconciliation.

"Charles, before I come back to you I must be completely honest. About Robbie, I…"

"Please do we have to talk of it more."

"We do. Because you may not want me back. I must be honest. Completely honest. About Robbie, I"

He looked at her with a blank stare.

Her hands began to tremble.

"Try as I may, and God knows I've tried, I still can't forgive you for taking him to the mill." Her fingers squeezed her brows. "I've relived it over and over and I just can't do it. It's horrible not to be able to forgive, I know. But I just can't."

He stared into a space that was beyond her and was silent a time.

You know I promised myself I would never bring it up again, but since we are trying to start over with as clean a slate as possible, I can't forgive you either. For running off with Dante Ravelli and leaving Robbie, even though I keep trying to believe you didn't know the extent of his illness."

"I swear to you I didn't or never would have left him if I had known."

He did not respond.

"And so perhaps these things lie too deep within us to reconcile," she finally said.

He sat up from the bed.

"Good God, no! Don't say that. We have to try to stop living in the past. The slate isn't completely clean, but, in time, perhaps we will learn to forgive."

"And you're willing to accept me back knowing how I feel?"

"Of course."

"Yes. Yes, I want to begin again, Eleanor. I think I can make you happy. Somehow you seem to have discovered my other flaws, the—drinking—and the neglecting of my obligations to the mill. If you can forgive that, that's enough for me right now."

"I'm so glad we've really talked, Charles. Got everything out in the open. It was the only way. It's for the best."

"You're right. As hard as it is to talk about, these things had to be said so we can work on them."

"In a few days you'll be going home."

He frowned half heartedly.

"You're wrong there. In a few days we'll both be going home."

When would this horror end? It continued into October. Schools were closed down weeks now, as were theatres and churches. Indoor meetings of any kind were banned and all church services were held outside for the few who ventured out with the courage and faith to do so. So many workers essential to running of the city became infected, and the employees at the telephone and telegraph company were out with the contagion in droves. Companies having skeleton work forces, including the telephone and telegraph companies, took out ads, imploring customers to cut out unnecessary calls and not request an operator unless absolutely essential. Doctors were at the point of exhaustion, often caring for four to nine sick patients in the same family.

Dr. Belli, their mainstay, who practiced at St. Joseph's but often visited the Alliance when Mary needed a consultation, succumbed to the flu himself. A pall hung over the Alliance when news of his passing reached them and spread throughout Paterson at the thought a doctor could die. The news account of his passing said he had administered to approximately two thousand patients the month before he died.

The pandemic worsened even more as it spread across the states. Eleanor read in the papers one of the most tragic deaths occurred in Illinois at Camp Grant. The colonel there, a Colonel Hagedorn, committed suicide over his heartbreak from losing so many men. Yet another account told of the father of some soldiers who were in different camps. He arrived at the first and his son had died. He went immediately to the next camp to comfort his second son. He was also dead. And then he found that the third had died at Camp Grant.

Eleanor vowed she would stop reading such accounts. They only succeeded in breaking her heart. Yet, she could not stop wanting to find out what was happening concerning the contagion's spread.

She read that in New Mexico a woman named Clara Garduno was the first in that state to succumb. The doctor, overworked to exhaustion, quickly pronounced her dead. Health Department officials demanded she be buried immediately to prevent the spread of the disease. Her husband secured the services of an undertaker. Because three of her children were also very ill at the time and not expected to survive, her grave was left uncovered to allow prompt burial of the children as soon as they too died. Two passed on the next day, and as the undertaker began to bury them the husband, Frank Garduno, asked to see his wife's body one last time. To his horror he discovered she had not been dead at the time she was buried, seeing signs she had clawed at the coffin. In his fear and haste to bury victims and stop the contagion, the doctor's pronouncement was incorrect. She had been buried alive, only then to suffocate.

Eleanor threw the newspaper across the room.

"I've had it! I will not read these accounts anymore. I can't bear it."

Charles, still pale, sat quietly on his bed.

"You should stop reading them. I believe it will run its course soon. I truly do."

He was correct.

By November the epidemic burned out. The disease finally relented, leaving countless families with shreds of lives.

And by November Charles was ready to return home with Eleanor.

Yes, she was home.

Their beginning days together were awkward, as though they were newlyweds. Charles appeared hesitant to say anything untoward and Eleanor felt the same.

But that soon changed.

"The UTW I'm told has enrolled most of the city's ribbon weavers and over fifteen hundred broad silk weavers. Can you believe that? And no relenting."

Eleanor stopped stirring her tea. "Do you realize how much power they'll have if there's a strike?"

"The textile workers are the smart ones. There's been so much in- fighting in the more radical unions they had to do something about it. And they did. Their organizers are experienced and can offer them a return for the hard-earned money they pay in dues. I can't blame them for uniting. You know," he said in hesitation, "I've had a great deal of thinking time with this flu hitting me and I've made a decision. One I hope you'll agree with."

"A decision?"

"I want to sell the mill."

"But what would you do? How would we manage?"

"I think we can get a good price for it. Catholina Lambert showed an interest when I broached the subject last Thursday night at our monthly meeting at the Bellevue. And I know Jack Carlson and John Flanagan would jump at the chance to buy it. I've tried to be a fair- minded owner and the workers have produced well. Not to mention how well our commission weaving has worked out, thanks to your encouragement." He looked wistful. "That seems so long ago, doesn't it?"

"We'd—sell the house?"

"Yes. I want to start over. For many reasons." His eyes misted. "Truthfully, there are too many memories here. For both of us. And, God knows, struggle as I do each day, I can't seem to overcome them. Each time I pass Robbie's room—"

"Please, Charles…"

"Forgive me. We could get a lovely home in Paterson's East Side section. Certainly not this elaborate. But I see ads now and then for these smaller mansions on Broadway."

She laughed.

"Have you forgotten I lived most of my life in a tenement, so, yes, a smaller mansion would be quite acceptable. In fact, a lovely house for me to decorate would do. But it must have lots of land for a large garden."

"That goes without saying." He took a sip of his coffee. "Well, then, it's settled. I'll formally announce it at the meeting I have with the mill owners next month. And we'll take it from there."

"How much did your father pay for this home?"

"I have no idea."

Before he could stop her, she was walking to the large armoire to get the box at the back shelf that held all their personal documents. She leaned forward, startled by what she saw lying behind it.

Three bottles of whiskey, one almost empty.

Charles flew from his chair.

"Let me—"

She grasped the box, thought quickly, smiled broadly.

"The papers should be in there."

She could see a sigh of relief on Charles' face. He quickly closed the armoire.

"I'll search for the documents and put the box back. I don't want you being bothered by such things." He placed his arm around her. "So it's settled then. About selling."

"Of course. Yes. We must start a new life."

She realized that now more than ever.

There was a small mansion for sale on Broadway. Though it needed work on the inside, Eleanor didn't mind.

She enjoyed decorating. But it was the garden that won them over, expanding at least three acres. Even though winter was approaching, she could imagine what the now-shriveled masses of hydrangeas that bordered both sides of the property must look like in bloom. And she immediately examined the myriad dormant rose bushes, black- eyed Susans, forsythia, echinacea, hosta, iris, phlox, so many other dead-looking bits of stems which excited her, for she could envision their flowering come spring and summer. Though the garden was unkempt in parts—the iris, for example, needed much dividing, and the mulching was not fully completed, this made sense after the realtor explained its owner, a sweet, elderly woman who had a son in California anxious to sell, died of a massive stroke. The house had been up for sale months now. She looked forward to putting the garden in order for it gave order to her sense of being. It seemed to be a way for her to challenge life itself. Though it seemed dead through most of fall and winter, it always sprang up victorious in spring. As long as she had a garden, she felt a sense of a future, and that sense gave her a feeling that life could be good. The seller was a surgeon and wanted to settle the estate as quickly as possible. He accepted their offer immediately. And so, along with the wonderful property, they bought the estate for much less than they expected to pay.

All appeared to be going well. They sold the house to one of Paterson's silk barons, John Flanagan, a craggy-faced man who bid highest for it, and his wife, a pinch-faced woman who was more interested it seemed in the gardens and appeared the type of woman who would cherish them as Eleanor had.

She did not cry the last day she walked through the rooms and garden on Silk Road one last time. She felt the burden of so much sorrow the house carried with it, especially the death of her child, the betrayal of the woman she thought her dearest friend, so much else, lifted from her shoulders and looked forward to a new beginning.

She felt nothing could be worse than the suffering she and Charles had known there.

Beads of sweat broke out on Charles' forehead that January of 1919 when he read the morning papers. The 18th Amendment had passed. Prohibition. No manufacturing, selling or consuming of alcohol.

Eleanor noticed Charles' shocked look.

"What's the matter?"

"Oh—my investments. A down turn."

"The companies will improve again. You know they always do. You've been very wise in your investments." "Of course they will."

"You're sweating. I hope it's not the return of—"

"The flu burned itself out. You know that. It's nothing. I just feel a bit warm. It's nothing." He wiped his forehead. "No fever, I assure you."

Charles retreated as soon as possible to his study. He had so much unpacking still before him, but his mind could only focus on one thing. His next drink. He had known for quite a time he could not get through his life without alcohol. He had always been a casual drinker, but his drinking had increased when his father died and held for him the terrifying task of taking over the mill. Even in death, it seemed his father's ghost hovered over him, challenged him to succeed, prove him wrong, be the kind of son he always wanted, not the quiet, introverted coward he felt his father saw him as, a man whose foolish passion was landscape architecture and gardens. And then, of course, he believed himself a murderer. If he hadn't taken his child to the mill where he'd contracted the virus from diphtheria…

He drank two shots of whiskey. Prohibition. He must find a way to get more. It was then that he thought of Stephen Kosinski, his former mill supervisor, his possible savior, a man with whom he had little in common, except for those wonderful nights they'd spent at various bars, drinking themselves to oblivion as he tried to blot out the past.

He called Kosinski.

He sounded somewhat secretive.

"Meet me at the back door of Jamison's Funeral Parlor at nine tonight."

"Why in God's name would I do that? It's not dead bodies I want to get my hands on. It's alcohol."

"Just do as I say. And bring your empty briefcase."

Befuddled as he was, he trusted Kosinski.

And he was a desperate man.

The alleyway leading to the back of the funeral parlor was dark, the owner having chosen to keep its lights off, which seemed odd to Charles. He met up with Kosinski who knocked on the back door, lightly.

A small, bald-headed man opened the door, his face reminding Charles of a squirrel's.

"We came to view the body," Kosinski said. "What's the name of the deceased?"

"Sean Fitzgerald Ferguson."

The man opened the door, let them in, closed it quietly, led them down a dark hallway to a heavy wooden door, knocked four times.

"Who's there?" A man's voice sounded muffled.

"Two men. Want to see Sean Fitzgerald Ferguson."

The man opened the door. A wave of bright light fell upon them. At least twenty men and a few women were in the room, some on couches, some on chairs, some sitting at bar stools. Two women were dancing the Charleston to loud music, beads around their neck flipping to and fro, their beautiful nylon-stockinged legs and bodies gyrating. They could easily have given Charles an erection in any other circumstance for he felt they were like lewd quasi-burlesque performers in their low-cut dresses, breasts bobbing up and down. But the sight of them paled when he saw the set up of patrons standing at the bar. He became mesmerized by the glorious, amber liquid flowing into their glasses. Before he knew it the bartender poured it into a glass and gave it to him. He felt the comfort of the liquor seeping through him in no time, more wonderful than victory, wealth, success, sex. He drank until he was satisfied. So did Kosinski.

He plopped money on the bar and bought four bottles of whiskey, which he placed in his briefcase. He knew Eleanor would be asleep as usual when he arrived home and he could hide them. He felt great elation at his good fortune.

"I can never thank you enough, Steve." He frowned. "I know I'm hooked on it, but I can't stop. It's my life blood now. God help me."

Kosinski sighed, "As if I couldn't understand that, my man."

"To know we have this source of it. With prohibition. Good God, I'm overjoyed."

They parted amicably, vowing to stay in touch.

Eleanor heard the clock downstairs chime two and Charles still had not arrived home. She dared not think of what might be the reason. She was confident he was faithful to her. Always. But when she saw the liquor hidden in back of the armoire she still did not want to face the reality of his drinking problem. Yet, it made sense. When he arrived at the Women's Alliance thin as a thread, she assumed it was because he was still punishing himself over Robbie's death and her leaving him. But surely he would not have stopped eating to such emaciation and in such a dramatic fashion unless, as she sadly accepted now, he was replacing his need for food with alcohol more and more.

Still, the following weeks she continued to rationalize his actions. His still meager eating at dinner might be based upon his slow recovery from the influenza virus. Loss of appetite was not uncommon in recovery. At first. Or perhaps he felt stress at no longer following his daily routine at the mill and his uncertainty about what he wanted to do with his life.

Through it all, she tried hard to show her support of him. Perhaps he still might not believe she would stay. And always the memory of their child haunted him, she knew, as it did her.

She began to question her own motives. Had she returned to him too soon? Was it pity, not love, that moved her to return when she thought he might die during the influenza outbreak? Was it because she finally realized Dante would never return to her? More and more, in her heart she realized Dante was a man who was unobtainable. Then why did she fall in love with him? What was it in herself that led her to choose a man whose whole life was to help the poor and truly unavailable to her completely?

She heard the key turning in the latch, listened as Charles tiptoed up the stairs, heard a few stumbles. She turned in bed to face the wall, pretending sleep. It would make no sense to confront him now in the condition he was in.

She would wait until the time seemed right.

It was a blessing for Eleanor to go to the Women's Alliance that morning, at least she thought so, until she saw Mary, red-eyed from crying, so uncharacteristic of her. She was a woman of such strength; yet, here she was, sitting in her office wiping her eyes and staring into space.

"They brought in Ann Dodge last night."

Mary attempted to compose herself, straighten her uniform. Mary had met Ann a few years back when the suffragist movement was emerging in England. She told Eleanor how they survived so much together, including being force fed with tubes down their throats to protest the injustices perpetrated against women. It was soon after her sojourn in England Mary decided to return to Paterson, her childhood home, and open the Women's Alliance. Ann returned as well and started her own small clinic in Bayonne. They seldom saw each other, both so dedicated to their life's work of serving the poor, but corresponded regularly.

"It's horrible." Eleanor noticed Mary's hands shook as they spoke. "She and her parents requested she be brought here because they felt the closeness of our friendship might help. But I worry St. Joseph's might be better under these circumstances. I've put her in the back area in Section 3."

"But surely we can help her. Or get help from St. Joseph's. What in the world is wrong with her?"

"An illness I have no knowledge of."

"And St. Joseph's does?"

"Her legs are paralyzed. And there's a new doctor there who deals with problems like this. They say they come from the mind. It's such a new field."

"The mind?"

"Her legs are stiff, immovable. But they can't find a physical reason. And her eyes. Good God. So sad, and she just seems to stare into space much of the time."

"It can't be possible. There has to be a physical reason for it."

Eleanor turned, began to walk towards the area of Ann Dodge's bed.

"I have to see this myself."

"I must warn you—"

But Eleanor kept walking. She did not want to doubt Mary's observations. Yet, she did. Quite possibly Miss Dodge had an undiscovered viral infection. It was absolutely impossible for her not to manifest some sort of symptom indicating a clue to her paralysis. And, of course, for some unknown reason, she could be faking.

She turned the corner and entered the area where Ann Dodge lay.

She became lightheaded at what she saw. She grasped the nearest bed railing, gasped for breath. Standing with his back facing her, was Dante Ravelli. The dark hair worn longer at his neck, the powerful build, the arms she had embraced so often… Dante. The man who possessed her love for so long she had practically annihilated herself, her own needs, she was so overcome by the passion she felt for him.

Memories she constantly tried to forget flooded her. The time she sat in her ragged coat in the freezing rain the first time he befriended her, the strength that emanated from him when he made his speeches during the IWW silk strike that nearly caused the workers to starve to death and had accomplished little. Then when he returned to Bayonne and the one against the Rockefellers. Her leaving Charles and her child. For him. Finally, her realization after so long she would never be his first love. The poor, the labor movement, justice—they were his life and first loves.

But why had he returned from Russia where he had gone to fight for the Revolution?

He turned.

She stared, speechless.

"You look pale, miss. Are you all right?"

Still she could not speak.

This was not Dante. This man had gray eyes, a hawkish nose, cheeks that looked sculpted of stone.

"I—"

He grabbed a chair.

"Sit down."

"I'm—I'm sorry. I thought you were—someone else."

"Someone you know well, no doubt?"

She looked at the floor.

"Yes. He left for Russia and I never expected to see him again."

"Ahhh…the shock." He extended his hand. "I'm Aaron Kirov. I'm replacing Dr. Belli for the time being. Dr. Lafferty asked me to come over and examine Miss Dodge."

He scrutinized her chart as he spoke.

"I don't believe I've ever seen you here before."

"This is my first visit. They still haven't been able to find a full- time doctor with their specific needs. But the patients must be served. I'm glad to oblige when I can, though my specialization is psychiatry. And I must admit I wish I could devote my full time to that."

"And you're visiting Ann Dodge?"

"Yes. I believe she is experiencing emotional trauma affecting her to the point she can not walk. Hysteria."

"But she's not hysterical at all." Eleanor felt impatience with such a diagnosis.

"This has nothing to do with outbursts of tears or acting out hysterically. Basically, it's when a person reacts with a physical manifestation to a mental problem she can not face. In her case, her reaction is paralysis of her legs."

"I find that impossible to believe. That the mind can cause the body to react in such a way." She stared directly into his eyes. "In fact, I think it's quite foolish. I'm inclined to think it's from an unknown virus or that she's faking for some reason."

"I understand your disbelief. This is such a new field in America, psychiatry. May I try to convince you she is not faking?"

"Of course. But I don't believe you can, if I may say so."

He smiled. "You certainly say what you think and feel, don't you? That metal pin you are wearing that identifies you as Eleanor Lafferty—"

"Please excuse me. I didn't introduce myself."

"May I borrow it?"

She hesitated, then handed it to him. He dipped its tip into the alcohol bottle on the tray beside them, and they moved to Ann Dodge's bed.

"Good morning, doctor."

Ann Dodge looked drawn and pale.

"Good morning, Miss Dodge."

Before Eleanor knew what was happening, he lifted her blanket and jabbed the pin in her thigh. She did not wince or move. He jabbed it into one or two other parts of her legs. She appeared oblivious to the pain.

Eleanor stood wide-eyed.

"I must apologize. No one could fake—"

"No need. But do you see? Her mind is doing this to her. Not her body. And we must find the reason."

"I'd never have believed—"

"It's quite understandable. This is not your field. And so new here, of course. Have you ever heard of Sigmund Freud?"

She remembered once Charles had mentioned this Sigmund Freud when she was having constant nightmares. She stiffened at the thought of them.

"Freud believes part of cure can come if we can understand and analyze our dreams and childhood experiences, confront them, bring them to the surface—"

She began to tremble thinking of the acts of abuse she'd known at the hands of the man she believed to be her father.

"Are you sure you're all right? Please. Sit down."

She did. She realized he sensed something was troubling her.

"I've heard of this Sigmund Freud."

"Have I upset you? Brought back a memory?"

"Of course not." How could she tell him about her having been sexually abused as a child?

"The field of psychoanalysis is much more prevalent in Europe, growing by leaps and bounds. Patients whose illnesses were considered hopeless have been helped using Freud's techniques. And of course," he hesitated, his voice gentle, "if I can help you in any way—"

"I have no need for such help, I assure you." She could feel herself blushing. "None. But if it can help my patients in any way, even a few, I want to learn more about it."

"I would hope the Paterson library will have some of his books. And if the library doesn't carry them, let me know. I'll give you mine to read."

"Oh, I couldn't—"

"Of course you could. You can't know how happy I am to know you are interested in this relatively new field. It will be my pleasure. I suppose I'll be seeing you now and then until further notice since I'll be here often and happy to collaborate with Dr. Lafferty. I've heard nothing but good reports about her."

They shook hands.

"You'll let me know about the books then."

"I will."

"Good day, Miss Lafferty."

"It's Mrs. Lafferty."

Had she seen a momentary spark of disappointment in his eyes?

"Forgive me. Mrs. Lafferty then."

He left soon after talking with Ann Dodge.

She felt unnerved. For something indefinable had passed between them.

Kirov found himself wondering about her, her past loves, her history with her husband. Was their marriage a good one? Then why did he see an expression of sadness in her eyes when he saw her? Was there something in her past affecting her now? Perhaps he could gain her confidence, slowly but surely, and figure out the mystery of this woman. He wondered why he should be so concerned. He rationalized that would be the case with any potential patient.

Aaron Kirov remained true to his word about the Alliance as well as Ann Dodge specifically. He visited intermittently, as Dr. Belli had, for consultations with Mary regarding any questions she might have and always stopped to see Ann Dodge. How Eleanor wished she could be privy to their conversations, but he had requested screens be placed around the area and Mary obliged. What kind of questions could a doctor ask that would cure a patient who, it seemed to Eleanor, had been physically paralyzed? She still could not accept Kirov's premise that her mind was the cause of her affliction.

As the weeks passed it seemed she was right. Ann Dodge remained in worse condition than she had been in a few months earlier when she was admitted.

"I'm frantic over this," Mary confided to Eleanor. "I don't know where to turn."

"I don't believe we'll ever be able to explain it. Maybe it's some type of virus that hasn't been discovered yet." She placed her hands on Mary's shoulder. "There must be millions of them, I'm sorry to say, that we most likely know nothing of."

"I just refuse to accept she'll be paralyzed this way for life. I just can't. And now she seems to be eating less, a sign she's becoming more disillusioned."

They watched Dr. Kirov from across the room as he removed the screen that surrounded Ann Dodge's bed.

"I never did apologize for not forcing myself to stop you, warn you, that first day Kirov arrived. When I saw him from behind I truly thought I was seeing a reincarnation of Dante Ravelli."

Eleanor's eyes misted. How often had she wondered about Dante, foolishly thought he would write her. But she must accept the fact he never had. She envisioned him in the midst of fighting with the Russian people for justice during the Revolution. More than likely he had met another woman with similar beliefs who had replaced her in his heart. Acceptance. That was what she must learn…

She changed the subject as quickly as possible.

"This Kirov. Tell me about him. What do you know? This outlook he has on the causes of certain illnesses."

"Little to nothing I'm afraid. Though I've tried to find out from the doctors and staff at St. Joseph's when I've been called over for consultation. Seems to be a loner. He's very close-mouthed about himself. Though his credentials are impeccable." Mary whispered, "I sneaked a look at them in the files when no one was around. I must say the rumors surrounding him intrigue me. Not only his theories about Freud. The file said he was born in Russia and later his family immigrated to Austria. He became a medical doctor and attained a degree with highest honors. Then for some reason something must have changed his life and his goals, and he began to study this psychiatry. He even studied with Freud for a time. I wonder what his wife must have thought of that, if he has one. To give up such a well-paying position and go into this strange, new field. Then it was stranger still when I saw that he left blank the section whether he was or wasn't married. There was not one personal notation by him on the form, even the section on why he wanted to work at St. Joseph's. And yet they hired him. He must surely be outstanding in his field."

"He is quite mysterious."

Eleanor too found him intriguing and had taken Freud's book on dream interpretation out of the library after asking the librarian to order a copy. It was rather scarce and hardly known, though Mary knew of some of his work. Eleanor found so much of it difficult to understand. She had spent so much of her time reading and trying to educate herself through the books Charles recommended, especially at the beginning of their marriage, but this one's content proved a challenge for her.

She glanced across the room at Ann Dodge. "I don't see much progress there."

Mary frowned. "Neither do I. Yet, somehow having read what I have by this Freud I'm not entirely the disbeliever I was before. He cites cures giving examples from some of his cases for what I believe is Ann's problem, hysteria."

Eleanor went back to work changing dressings, taking temperatures, changing beds, administering medications, disinfecting. So much to do. Lately she found herself staying longer periods at the Alliance, hoping she would have less time to cope with Charles. She knew she could no longer ignore the situation she found herself in and must face him and his drinking problem.

She made her decision at that moment. She would confront him.

Tonight.

She waited for the sound of Charles' footsteps that evening. She surveyed the room to calm herself. The various touches she had been adding with her decorating pleased her. As she did on Silk Road, she had chosen a light palette. Even in winter it would give a joyful, airy feeling to the rooms. She needed to be surrounded by bright color which made the dark moods that often assaulted her more and more more bearable. Lately, it seemed that some days she regretted every new breath. And the new wallpaper of her bedroom strewn with roses lifted her heart. Part of the stipulation of the sale of the Silk Road house was that she be allowed to take the French-tiled fireplace that decked her bedroom with its floral screen as well.

She went to the library, began to pace the room, then realized Charles was already home and lay half asleep in his chair, facing the fireplace. She breathed deeply, regained her composure.

She shook him gently. He immediately opened his eyes.

"Charles, we have to talk."

"What is it? Are you all right?"

"Of course I'm all right. It's you I'm worried about."

He rubbed his eyes. "I'm sorry, my dear, I'm not feeling so well."

"For the past months?"

She met his look head on.

"When are you going to decide what to do with your life now that the mill is sold? You just can't sit around all day like this. Heaven knows, there's still so much to be done with the unpacking alone. So many of our things are still sitting in boxes after all this time. And your future. You don't seem to have given any thought to that as well."

"I can't say I blame you for being angry. I promise—I really will try to get something done with more unpacking tomorrow."

"And then what? The rest of your life?"

"You know we have no monetary worries. We made a wonderful profit on that house with all that land. Plus the money my father left me. And the sale of the mill. So why worry so? We're set for life. I must admit I've also made some sound investments as well."

"That's not the point. It's what you're going to do with your life, what will give you some purpose, that I'm—

"I've been thinking about that. I have. And I've got a few ideas."

"Well, for heaven's sake, share them with me."

"I thought—perhaps something like landscape architecture. You know it's always interested me."

"But wouldn't that mean going back to school again?"

"I'm certain it would. But it's just a thought."

"Is that where you've been going nights then? To discuss ideas with friends about landscape architecture?" She could not disguise the sarcasm in her voice.

His face flushed. "Well, I have been meeting a few friends—at the Bellevue—to talk about various topics. The strikes, our new home, memories about the mill. It seems the past is not as out of my system as I expected it would be."

She sighed.

"Thank heavens. I was beginning to think it was— something else. Another woman, perhaps," she lied.

He rose from his chair, encircled her in his arms.

"Eleanor, there will never be another woman for me. I love you more than my own life." He smiled. "Do I sound dramatic?"

She smiled, "Please, keep sounding dramatic. It sounds wonderful." She held him tighter.

He released her slowly. "I'm afraid I do have to get out again tonight. Not for too long. Steve Kosinski's mother died and he's so distraught, as you can imagine. I can't not go to the wake. You understand."

"Of course. How sad. He's a good man. You must send my sympathy."

"I will.

"I'm just not up to going."

Moments flashed before her when her mother died in her arms. She could almost smell the scent of Ivory Soap emanating from her as she held her that last time.

And Charles. There for her. Always there for her…

She just could not approach the subject of his drinking, the liquor in the armoire. And perhaps, she rationalized, Kosinski's mother had died. She refused to allow herself to see beyond Charles and his goodness.

"Are you all right? I hope I haven't upset you. A sad thing, I know."

"I'm all right."

He kissed her then and left to meet Kosinski. He despised himself at how adept he had become at being such a liar. Landscape architecture? Meeting the mill owners at the Bellevue? The ruling part of him now made him tremble with his need for that amber liquid, that blessed comfort he would experience when he drank it down and it permeated him. He must have it. He knew it was too late for him to give it up. It was his life blood now.

Ann Dodge made no progress. In fact she worsened, eating less and less. Eleanor could not help but admire Kirov for his ceaseless efforts, many times staying longer than his allotted hours. He barely said hello to her, and she was beginning to convince herself she imagined something had passed between them. Yet, why did she wish he would at least acknowledge her with more than a nod or brief smile?

Then one day he knocked her off balance when she happened to be passing him to get some syringes adjacent to the area where Ann Dodge lay. He grasped her just in time or she surely would have fallen. She felt a surge of sexual energy bolt through her. And from the look in his eyes as he held her those momentary seconds she knew he felt it too. When she quickly gained her balance, he let her go as though he had touched a searing iron.

"I—forgive me, Mrs. Lafferty. I—"

"There's nothing to forgive. It was my fault. I should have been watching where I was going." She straightened her uniform. "How is Ann Dodge faring, Dr. Kirov? Any progress at all?" Why had she made certain she addressed him as Dr. Kirov? Why must she make sure theirs was only a professional relationship?

He frowned.

"I'm sorry to say she isn't progressing at all. There is a key to all this, but I just can't seem to unlock the door."

"Well, you've certainly done your best. Twelve visits now you've been trying."

"Have you counted the visits?"

She blushed. "Why, no, I was just guessing."

"Well, you are right. Because I have counted. Counted the times because I will see you as well. You must pardon me. I am too forward. But nevertheless, it is true."

"I don't think we should continue this conversation." She turned abruptly. "I should get started clearing a wider path to Miss Dodge's bed and get Brigitte and Nora to help me."

"Why is that may I ask?"

"Her father rarely visits. But he's visiting today. He called Dr. Lafferty this morning to inform her. He's in a wheelchair, you see, and we have to maneuver the beds so—"

"A wheelchair? He's in a wheelchair?"

"Why, yes."

He clasped her hand a brief moment.

"You've told me something that may be very important."

"I don't understand."

"I must go to patients at St. Joseph's." He smiled at her. "But I'll return soon. That will be my thirteenth visit."

She studied him as he walked to the door. He turned briefly, waved goodbye to her.

And then he was gone.

Kirov hoped his theory about Ann Dodge and her illness was right. For then he would not have to visit the Alliance as often, for he found himself being more and more attracted to Eleanor Lafferty, and this could not be. Yet, he wished he could help her. The glazed look she often had in her eyes, the fatigue she often showed for no reason, the depressed demeanor she often showed, symptoms he could notice immediately. Perhaps someday she would tell him about her past, but he doubted it.

Kirov kept his promise and returned the next day. He smiled at Eleanor when she entered the room.

"I was wondering," he hesitated, "I—well—you seem interested in Freud's work, and I thought perhaps you might want to observe me today. Of course, nothing may happen. And if you don't feel—"

"I would be honored, I assure you. I'm open to every avenue possible if it can help a patient."

"As I said, nothing may happen. Nothing at all." He squeezed his chin. "It is hard not to be discouraged. Not to give up. Sometimes I feel that way."

"You're too hard on yourself. I sense you are a great idealist." She smiled. "And that's what makes a great doctor."

He held the curtain back for her, and she entered the area where Ann Dodge lay. Her skeletal form seemed lost beneath her blanket, a tiny skull protruding above it.

"Miss Dodge, do you mind if Mrs. Lafferty observes with me today?"

"No." Her voice was nearly inaudible.

"I understand your father visited this morning. After all our conversations about him, you never mentioned he was in a wheelchair."

"Is that important? I don't see how it can be."

"You told me you received a marriage proposal from a man you love very much. Forgive me if I restate some of these points, but I am trying to fill in Mrs. Lafferty on the situation."

"Of course."

"And you love him dearly. Yet, your father never approved of him."

"I don't know why. He has a very high standing position in the government. And he is so kind." She smiled. "And handsome."

"I've seen him visit many times," Eleanor offered.

"And was it about this time you became unable to walk?"

"Yes. That is why I can't understand it. I love them both with my whole heart."

"And your father? You've cared for him for years, haven't you? He's entirely dependent upon you. A widower, as I remember? And you're his only child. Do you know what I think? I think the conflict between taking care of your paralyzed father has transferred to you. Your legs, feet. Where his paralysis lies. Perhaps at first you felt an emotional paralysis. How could you leave your father? He needs you so. Surely you must have been in severe distress at having to leave him. Yet, you had lost your heart to—Johan is it?—and your mind, you see, stepped in and gave you a way out."

She grasped his hands tightly.

"Your mind has played a trick on you. If you became paralyzed physically as well as emotionally, as I believe is true, your conflict does not have to be faced."

"But my feet? My legs? Why am I paralyzed there?"

"Where is your father's paralysis?

"His—legs."

She did not speak a time, what seemed an eternity. She stared at Kirov a long time, as did Eleanor. Could this be true? That a conflict in the mind could actually cause a physical manifestation such as this?

"Now," he spoke softly, "you won't have to decide. You are also paralyzed. Plus all the years of care you have devoted to him can be no more if you marry. Your paralysis has become a solution, relieving you of guilt. You don't have to decide to marry Johan now and leave your father, break his heart, as you see it. Yet, you love Johan. Instead, you are breaking your own heart. And if you choose not to make a decision between your father and Johan, you will continue this way I fear."

Ann Dodge and Eleanor remained silent. Time passed. Kirov took Ann Dodge's hand in his.

Eleanor approached closer to the bed.

"I have no right to speak, I know, Miss Dodge, but if you love this man—Johan—as he loves you, there is nothing more important than that love. And your happiness with him. Please. Don't sacrifice your life caring for your father. Perhaps he can get a live-in nurse. There are always solutions to such things. I'll help you find one. And, of course, you can visit him often. It's time now for you to have happiness in your own life." She felt her eyes misting. "But love. If you feel that for him as he does for you, don't let it slip away. Without love, life means nothing. And you are blessed to have it."

She turned to leave.

"Mrs. Lafferty!"

Eleanor turned to her. Kirov's face paled. Both were taken aback by what they saw. Ann Dodge's blanket was moving. Slowly. Kirov quickly threw the blanket back. He and Eleanor stood, breathless. They watched as she moved her toes.

They sat on the bed.

"I understand." She turned to Eleanor. "Oh, how you have helped me."

Eleanor smiled. "I think Dr. Kirov had something to do with it as well."

"Doctor, forgive me. Of course. Of course!" She held out her arms to him as he sat down next to her and hugged him. "You saved my life."

"On the contrary. You have saved your life. I merely led you to the realization of the cause of the paralysis." He gently released her. "Well, let's get to it then. I want Dr. Lafferty to see your improvement, surprise her. Shall we try?"

"I'm not sure I can do this."

"Of course you can. Let me carry you. You're weak."

He pushed the curtain aside, lifted her, carried her to where Mary was taking a child's temperature. She finished, then looked up wide-eyed at seeing them.

"You know this young lady, I believe." Kirov smiled.

"Show her, Ann."

Ann wiggled her toes, moved her legs slightly.

"Ann! My God, it's a miracle."

"I'm afraid not," Kirov said. "Just a victory of the mind."

"You've convinced me," Eleanor said later and meant it. "I want to learn even more about these theories of Freud."

"I'm glad of it."

Mary beamed. "That makes two of us. Ann, you must tell me everything. Even what you think is the smallest detail of how this came about." She turned to Kirov. "We must talk later."

Eleanor and Kirov left them and she escorted him to the door, which she had not done before. She had the strongest desire to remain with him as long as possible.

"Did you mean it when you told Ann Dodge about the meaninglessness of life without love?"

"Of course I did."

"You are a fortunate woman then to have the love you described."

"That isn't what I said."

"Well, I assumed—"

"But what of you? I'm sure you look forward to seeing your wife beaming with love for you as you enter the door each evening."

His look darkened. "I'm afraid that is not the case."

"I must say you are quite mysterious. You must surely know that. I'm told by some of the nurses you never speak of your personal life." She half-smiled at him. "They call you their "mystery man.""

"Indeed? I had not realized that. It's just that I feel my personal life is just that and do not choose to share it. I was hired as a doctor and psychiatrist and try to fulfill those roles to the best of my ability."

She could not help but notice the clipped tone in his voice.

"I'm sorry if I've offended you."

"Of course you have not. And if you did, I assure you I would forgive you immediately."

He left soon after. She spent much of the afternoon tending to patients' needs but thinking of his words. Did he have a wife? He had not really said so. If so, were they separated? That was frowned upon by so many, but it certainly would have no effect upon St. Joseph's Hospital in hiring a qualified doctor. Or perhaps he wasn't married at all. But why hadn't he said it then?

Try as she might to dismiss the thought, she hoped the latter was true. She wondered about this. Why was she attracted to men who were unavailable to her? First Dante. Now Kirov. Did it have something to do with a flaw within her? She had been trying her hardest to understand Freud and wondered if her childhood experiences might have something to do with this, what Freud would say.

Eleanor could not wait until dinner was over and she could get into bed and try to read further to understand Freud's theories and hoped perhaps herself in part. Yet, when she got into bed she found it might have to wait until tomorrow she was so exhausted by the day's happenings. Ann Dodge was recovering by the power of mind. There was no doubt about it. That alone overwhelmed her, but the conversation with Kirov and the emotions it aroused in her made even Ann Dodge's recovery pale by comparison.

She must face it head on. She was uncontrollably drawn to this strangely attractive and intellectual man. She knew she must absolutely control this attraction. Yet, she felt such a desire within her, the same one she knew when she was with Dante Ravelli, who was also unattainable and duty bound. Well, she would surely not let it lead anywhere this time. She had learned her lesson well a few years ago when her great, idealistic love chose his work with the poor, suffering masses over her. She could envision him now, planning a revolt with the Russian peasants or sitting in some cafe with a group of workers or intellectuals. For months she hoped to hear from him, foolishly thinking a letter would come saying he loved her above all things and wanted to return. No letter arrived.

And then there was Charles. He was worthy of her love, adored her to distraction. When she left him so that both of them could come to grips with the death of their child and sort out their lives, she came to realize in her aloneness she truly missed him. His was a dependable love. She felt no regret returning to him, nursing him through the deadly flu. He must be her life now.

Aaron Kirov was a fleeting attraction. That was all.

PART II

Revelations

Colin McCarthy pulled his scarf tighter around his neck. It was colder than he expected on the Olivia, the ship that brought him back to America to his daughter, Eleanor. He remembered the first time he arrived, standing on the deck with Elizabeth, the woman who became Eleanor's mother, and her betrothed, Michael O'Bannion. She was also the woman he loved as well, though she did not realize it then, his love unspoken until years later when she returned that love.

And now. His eyes filled at the thought of Elizabeth's death, the terrible way she died, and hoped she had passed to that greater heaven she believed in so fervently. And Michael O'Bannion. If there were a hell, he surely would be burning there for his abuse of Elizabeth and Eleanor, which had still left her with such emotional scars.

He now knew Eleanor had suffered sexual abuse since she was five years old at the hands of her alleged father and held that secret in her heart. If only he had known he surely would have killed him. And then there was her beautiful child who had died. Yet, here she was, standing before him trying to look strong, glad to see him. Yet he sensed a sorrow in her eyes that held all the pain and suffering that had been in her life. If only he could give her a degree of happiness at his return, he would be a happy man.

He felt more and more certain he made the right decision leaving Ireland and returning to America. He knew in his heart he was thought a traitor to Ireland by his leaving. But with all the carnage he saw, he began to change. The senselessness of all that slaughter. The years of fighting in Ireland and America for the International Workers of the World and equal rights for the workers, he hated to admit, had worn him to the bone and also seemed hopeless.

And not a day went by he didn't think of Eleanor. He wanted to be with her in his last years, and, simply stated, wanted to end his days in peace.

He knew too he had to set one last thing straight, something that had gnawed at his conscience for years, for his own sake as well as Eleanor's. He felt sick with shame at the thought of it, that he had not revealed the secret festering in him all these years. Sick with guilt he had not even told Elizabeth about it.

But now it was time to make things right, and he could only hope for Eleanor's forgiveness.

Eleanor's excitement at the thought of seeing her father again sustained her, along with her work at the Women's Alliance. She stayed longer hours so she wouldn't have to encounter Charles, convincing herself it could not possibly be Kirov she hoped to see the longer evenings she spent there when after hours at St. Joseph's Kirov visited the few seriously ill patients Mary asked him to see.

One evening he came and appeared taken aback at seeing her at such a late hour. Try as she did to control herself, her heart somersaulted when he approached her.

He frowned. "I had not expected to see you here so late." "I could say the same to you."

"In truth, I thought it best to visit when you are not here if I possibly can." His voice sounded low, husky.

"What does that mean?"

"I think you know what that means. That I am attracted to you. I find it hard to function at times thinking of you." He smiled. "There. I've said it. Freud would be proud of me."

"We can't help being attracted to certain people." She clenched her hands behind her. "As long as we don't act upon it if it's forbidden."

She faced him squarely.

"You must stop coming here. Surely they can find another doctor. I'm afraid—of my feelings for you. Of what is happening."

"I have asked about a transfer back to St. Joseph's full time but they have refused me."

He looked at her intensely.

"Are you saying you feel the same way?"

She studied him, his steel gray eyes unnerving her.

"Yes."

"But you mustn't be afraid of it. You are absolutely right. As long as we don't act upon it. And I don't intend to. I must tell you—I am married as well. Though I never speak of it. And I trust you will not. So that is the end of it, you see—"

"Yet—"

He turned abruptly.

"Dr. Lafferty wants me to check and consult with her on three patients." She handed him their charts. "Perhaps you can direct me to them."

She brushed the front of her uniform and became a paragon of efficiency as she directed him to the first patient.

Mary stood in the doorway of her office, holding back tears. She knew the look of desire when she saw it, for she lived with that desire daily. She had been in love with Eleanor for such a long time. Who could not love a woman who possessed such courage through all the darkness she experienced in her life? Her near-starvation from the 1913 strike, how her heart must tumble every time a child was brought to the clinic, most likely bringing back memories of leaving her own child and self-blame, her separation, for better or worse, from Charles. But now at least they were together again.

But she knew her love for Eleanor was as forbidden as the one Kirov and she must be beginning to feel for each other.

Eleanor trudged home, her heart felt like pulp. Kirov had completely unnerved her. Her love for Dante Ravelli had nearly annihilated her selfhood. That would never happen again. Never. Charles needed her. She must be strong—and loyal to him.

She knew most likely he was in the library. She heard the radio playing "You Are Love," one of her favorites from *Show Boat*. Eleanor never ceased to be thrilled by this relatively new device, the radio, which comforted her greatly. To hear sound and music and people actually speaking to you and playing songs for you in your own living room! And Charles was just as addicted, although he preferred to hear about news events.

Strange… It was far too late for him to have waited for her for dinner.

She shook him hard and grasped a whiskey bottle from his hand.

"Charles!" The stench of whiskey emanating from his breath turned her stomach.

He opened his eyes, grabbed for the bottle.

"Give that to me!"

"No! You've had enough. Look at you."

He walked towards her, pushed her against the wall. Her shoulders and head felt as though a flame had touched them. Her face stiffened. Charles had never hurt her in any way before. She touched the back of her head, examined her hand, stained with blood. She trembled as she handed him the half-empty bottle.

She plopped down into the nearest chair.

Charles managed to get to the sofa, immediately drinking what was left in the bottle. In a few moments he tried to stand up but could not, fell against the corner of the living room table. Blood gushed from his forehead into his eyes from the gash he had caused, spurting on the rug.

This was beyond her ability to handle. She would call Mary. As she rushed toward the phone, she realized she could not. How could she let Mary see her adored brother in such a condition?

She must call someone she could trust. Charles was an important man in the community, and the love the workers felt for him remained steadfast, even after he sold the mill. His reputation must not be ruined. Most of the doctors at St. Joseph's were good friends of his and knew him well from his charitable involvements. She could destroy that image because he had become—she must face it—an inebriate.

Then it came to her. Kirov. She knew she could trust him. He was a loner, certainly not involved in any committee Charles was on.

She called St. Joseph's. "Is Dr. Kirov available? It's Eleanor Lafferty calling."

"I'll check for you."

In a few moments he was on the phone. "Kirov here."

"It's Eleanor. Can you come to my home right away? My husband's had—an accident—and needs a doctor."

She expected his next question to be why she hadn't called Mary, his sister. It was not.

"I'm on my way."

"It's 207 Broadway."

She was surprised how quickly he arrived. He surveyed Charles, attended to the gushing blood on his temple, then stitched and bandaged it.

"He'll be fine. He reeks of alcohol. That's what most likely caused him to stumble and fall. We have to try to get him to vomit. Do you have a basin? And please hurry."

Kirov held him down while Eleanor found a basin, put her finger down his throat as he vomited profusely and they got him to revive.

Kirov kept struggling with Charles' attempts to break away. He grasped his shoulders. "Don't be foolish. We're trying to help you." He vomited more. Finally, he stopped; then, in exhaustion, closed his eyes, fell back in a stupor. "He should be all right by morning."

They carried him to the couch and lay him there. Eleanor grabbed the afghan from another chair and covered him.

"He'll sleep it off now. You mustn't worry."

Kirov faced her squarely, noticed her hand, saw the blood on her fingers."

"Did he—hurt you?"

Still panic stricken, she acknowledged, "He threw me against the wall."

"Let me look at you. Do you feel pain in your shoulders? Head?"

"Yes, but I'll be all right."

He examined the back of her head and shoulders, bandaged the back area of her head. "You'll have pain for a time but I believe in a week or so you'll be fine. If the pain continues beyond then, you must let me know." He sighed heavily. "You must never argue with him when he's drunk. Do you hear me? He is a different person then and can be violent. Please promise me."

"Yes. Yes. I promise. You've been a great help. Why didn't I think to make him vomit?"

"You were in shock when you saw all that blood most likely. And his attacking you. Perhaps you didn't want to face the fact he drank so much he could hurt you and be another person, in a state of near alcohol poisoning."

She half smiled. "Freud would most likely say that, I suppose. Am I right?"

"Possibly."

"I'm so sorry but you have to deal with this situation. It's essential he gets help. The sooner the better. For your own safety as well."

"It's the first thing I'll bring up when he's sober again. Are there special places he can go for help, do you know?"

"I'll look into it if you like."

"I've been a fool. Looking the other way too long."

"I'm glad you chose me to call. It meant a great deal to me to have your trust."

"I feel—I know—you will be discreet."

"Of course."

She led him to the door. They faced each other, the look of desire covering their faces.

"Well, I thank you again."

She heard the clunking sound of his satchel as he placed it on the marble floor. She approached the door, clenched the knob. And then she felt his hand grasp her arm. He turned her to him, did not speak. She felt unspeakable desire flowing through her, tried to fight it with all her might. This could not, must not happen. Why was she always attracted to men she could never completely have? He was a married man. But it was too late. He was holding her in his arms, kissing her passionately, and she felt pierced by such emotion that she had to hold onto him to stand. And then she responded. His lips were warm. She could feel the power of his need as well as her own as he held her, both knowing their rapture would not be culminated.

Finally, with all the strength they could call upon, they separated.

"How I have dreamed of holding you in my arms, feeling the warmth of you. If it is wrong of me, so be it."

He bent down, grasped his satchel.

"What will become of us?" she finally managed to say.

"I don't know. I am as troubled as you are. But I believe destiny will have its say. Goodbye."

She watched him walk the path to his automobile, his head down. Why would she still tolerate a man who would hurt her so? What deep bond did she have with Charles, so deep she would stay with him? Did it have to do with their dead child? Some secrets of her past she was terrified to reveal and get help?

Eleanor tossed and turned most of the night. Fortunately, Charles was downstairs on the sofa. She could not stop thinking of Charles' hurting her and of Kirov, the desire she felt for him, his strange comment about their destiny. Surely they controlled their fate. And her instincts frightened her for they told her if she kept seeing him she might surely succumb to him. That must not happen. She could not endure the pain and suffering it would involve. Yet, there would be the greatest joy…

And what of Charles? A man who needed and deserved her complete support, the events that bound them together. By pure strength of will and the blessedness of helping others at the Women's Alliance, she realized she must go forward with her life after her child's death, her heart seeming to bleed in sorrow. How much longer could she hold herself together before falling apart? There was never a day she did not think of Robbie. Memories waited everywhere. Women who brought their infants to the clinic, the room in their new house where Robbie's clothing lay. She still could not discard the small brush she had used daily to brush his hair. Then there were his toys, his crib, other items. She had approached Charles saying perhaps they should discard these items or, at least store them in the cedar chest. He had finally agreed. Yet, now she found she could not do it.

She wondered if he had made a mistake in selling the mill after all. At least it would have given him a purpose. His plans to get a degree in landscape architecture never materialized. And so, she was certain he sat home most of the day while she was at the Women's Alliance, thinking, reliving the past, the fatal day he brought the baby to the mill where he most likely caught diphtheria, which killed him in the end.

She opened her eyes and to her surprise saw Charles standing before her, his suit a mass of wrinkles, blood stained, his head bandaged.

"How can you ever forgive me?" He sat down on the bed next to her.

"Tell me why I should."

"Because—because I'm a fool. And, God forgive me, I attacked you. I must have been out of my mind. I have the most wonderful wife in the world, and I go to the club—and come home drunk."

"Last night wasn't your club night. Please. Spare me your lies. You probably spent much of the night out somewhere drinking. Or maybe you stayed home, wallowed in self-pity, and drank here while I was at the Alliance. You can't go on like this. You have to try to move on, painful as it is for you. I won't stand for what's happening to you and me. I won't."

"One night of drinking too much and you're— "

"This has been going on a long time. I'm no fool. I just didn't want to believe it."

His face turned ashen.

"Do you want me to leave?"

"Of course not. I won't ask you to leave. Not at this point. You surely know that. But I have one condition for your staying."

"Which is?"

"That you get help. You won't admit you need it, I know. And I've chosen to ignore it too long. You've got a drinking problem. And we've got to face it."

He turned towards the mantel. "You're over reacting. I drink a bit too much once in a while. That's all."

"It isn't as simple as that. It was months back I saw those bottles of whiskey hidden in the armoire. But I stupidly chose to look the other way."

"I tell you—I swear to you—it isn't necessary I get help. I can do it on my own. It's as simple as that. This won't happen again."

She scrutinized him carefully. She guessed his face had reddened considerably from the shame he must have felt from their conversation and his attacking her. Should she give him another chance? What did Kirov know? He was not an authority on alcoholism. Yet, he was a doctor…

She sighed. "I don't know what to say. I really don't."

"Say you'll give me a chance to prove to you I'm right. It's over. I won't touch another drop of liquor. I swear it."

She did not speak a time. Weariness overcame her as she grasped the fireplace shelf, wondering how much strength she had left to call upon, how much of her heart she could hold together before it cracked.

"All right. All right. I'll give you one chance. I believe in you. I do. I know how life can sometimes be hell because of—the past. But to look to the future. So much depends upon you staying sober."

"I understand."

But did he? Did she? She truly meant their future relationship would depend upon his sobriety. But did she also mean the relationship she was tempted to have with Kirov also depended on it?

At that moment she made a decision. She realized she had no alternative but to leave the Women's Alliance to avoid seeing Kirov.

Dr. Mary Lafferty sat quietly in Dr. Howard Birnbaum's office. She knew she should have been sitting in that very place months ago. But she had so many patients to attend to, so much to do. She felt the lump in her breast around the time of the flu epidemic. But how in the world could she get it checked out then? She vowed she would when things calmed down somewhat at the Alliance. But they never did. And now the lump had grown so rapidly it was the size of a walnut. Every night she lay in bed touching it but then thinking of all the tasks that lay ahead the next day, the bandages that needed changing, the splints that most likely need to be applied, the medications that had to be carefully administered, the dressings changed, the onslaught of new patients, most from the silk mills. She was so grateful to Eleanor, a hard, efficient worker, along with Nora and Brigitte. But it was Eleanor who was at the core of the work. How could she function at any level without Eleanor by her side for she loved her to distraction?

Dr. Birnbaum was a paragon of efficiency as he tweaked his moustache and led her to his spotless office, then the examining room.

"Mary, I'm disappointed in you. You're a doctor, for God's sake. The size of this tumor is very large. Surely you must have noticed it way before now. Why did you wait so long to come to see me?"

"I didn't have the time."

"Spare me your excuses. You'll report to the hospital tomorrow and have it removed immediately. We've got to see—"

"Is it cancer?"

He frowned. "I don't know at this point."

"I'm not a fool. You've examined enough women to be able to give an educated guess."

"No, I won't. Not until we examine it further."

As he spoke, she saw a dark look flash across his face.

When Mary returned to the Alliance, she found Eleanor waiting in her office, having just arrived for the three o'clock shift. Her heart pounded harder when she saw Eleanor, as it always did.

"Mary, are you all right? You're always here."

"Of course I am. I just had a few chores to do."

"I need to talk to you."

"Right now? I'm behind with my work and thought perhaps you could give me an extra hand. I'd like to go home a bit earlier today." She rubbed her forehead. "I feel quite exhausted for some reason."

"You? Leave earlier?" Eleanor's concern was evident but she wanted to get her decision off her mind. "What I want to tell you won't take long."

"All right then."

"I've decided to leave the Alliance. As soon as possible."

Mary's heart thumped harder. Not to see her every day, at least to be near her. And now? The cancer she was convinced she had. She vowed not to tell her, but she had become aware of all the procedures at the Alliance she could almost take over with Dr. Kirov as consultant.

Mary sat down, clasped her arms over her clenched knees.

"I—must ask you to reconsider. I can't let you go now. You see, I need you to run the Alliance. Just briefly, I'm sure. I have to be away for a time."

"Away? Where are you going?"

"I had no intention of telling you this, but if it means you'll stay, hopefully—"

"Telling me what?"

"I have a—lump in my breast. I have to go to the hospital to have it diagnosed and removed. The sooner the better. And I'm sure I'll need some time to recuperate. Not long, most likely."

Eleanor felt lightheaded, sat down. "In your breast? Is it—cancer? But that's impossible. You know the signs. You'd surely have gone immediately—" Moments passed. Suddenly she clenched her hands to her face, began to cry, tears running through her fingers.

Mary rose, placed her hand on Eleanor's shoulder. "There now. You've always been a pillar of strength to me. You mustn't crumble now. Besides, we don't even know the diagnosis yet."

"He wasn't sure?"

"No. Of course he wasn't. It could be benign. Surely it is. I have to check into St. Joseph's tomorrow."

So soon. Eleanor was no fool. That could only mean one thing. She dared not face it. Mary meant the world to her. When she worked in the silk mill, it was Mary who encouraged her to leave and train at the Women's Alliance. She told Eleanor she believed she had the intelligence and sensitivity to be an excellent nurse. And it came to pass after she and Mary's brother, Charles, separated, nursing at the Alliance under Mary's guidance gave her selfhood back. She realized one reason she tolerated Charles' drinking so long was because she did not want Mary to ever find out about it. He was her idol. And Charles loved Mary so. What would her illness do to him? How could he ever focus on not stopping drinking if he found out Mary had cancer? What strength within him did he have left when he was so worn down by life?

Now leaving the Alliance was out of the question. She vowed to be there to help Mary in any way she could, no matter how much strength it would cost her. She was no fool. She sensed Mary loved her in a forbidden way. But it did not matter. She was certain Mary would never act on it, did not suspect Eleanor sensed her love and desire. She would be there for her no matter what happened.

And what of Kirov? She would have more contact than ever with him since he would probably visit more often with Mary absent. A doctor's presence would be even more essential at times.

What was it he said about their relationship? Something about destiny.

It seemed destiny's wheel had begun to turn.

Eleanor sat in the corridor of St. Joseph's Hospital waiting for information regarding Mary. She had insisted upon being with her to await the results of the surgery, much to Mary's protestations. She prayed she would not see Kirov. And now as she lifted her bowed head, he stood before her.

"Are you all right? What is it? Are you sick?"

"No. It's Mary. She's being operated on by Dr. Birnbaum. She has a tumor in her breast." She broke down in tears. "How will I ever get through life if anything happens to her, if it's terminal? I can't imagine a life without Mary. She's been such a friend and inspiration."

He sat down beside her, held her hand in his. "You're way ahead of yourself. It could be benign. And she's in good hands with Dr. Birnbaum. I respect him a great deal. Surely it must be very tiny. She's a doctor and knows to be aware of such things."

"It's quite large. She never takes care of herself. Always the patients. The Alliance. That's all she lives for. She's one of the most caring people you can imagine. And now"

He sat down, held her close. She felt the comfort of his arms as he tightened them around her. "There now. Let's wait before we jump to conclusions."

He released her. They sat quietly a few minutes.

"Do you mind my sitting here? I have patients waiting, but seeing you has taken me aback. You surely know that."

"I'm—glad you're here."

"Do you think we could ever meet outside the hospital setting? Only to share a cup of tea perhaps?"

"I—don't think so."

"Will you at least think about it? That's all I ask. You can't imagine how many hours I've spent trying to get the courage to ask you if you would go with me for a cup of tea." He smiled. "Quite ridiculous, no?"

"And how many hours I've spent hoping you would ask. And now I say no. What kind of sense does that make?"

"I understand."

"I'll think about it." She took his hand in hers impulsively. "I will."

"That's all I ask."

They both saw Mary wheeled into the hospital operating room at the same time.

"I'd better go. I doubt she wants to see me here right now." He rose. "Be strong."

He left her then, her heart in shreds as she watched him go.

Dr. Birnbaum gave Mary the results of the lump in her breast.

"It was cancer. Quite advanced and I removed a large portion of your breast. Hopefully, I got it all. But I must be honest. I may not have. We know little about these things. Hopefully, the day will come when we advance in knowledge."

"What is the prognosis?"

"I wish I could be exact. But I can't."

"When can I return to work?"

"Let's see how things work out first."

"But I must know."

"What you must do is rest and heal."

"If you—didn't get it all, based on your experience in this area and other similar operations on a tumor this size, how long do I have?"

"How can I answer such a question?"

"How long?"

He did not speak a time.

"I would like an answer. As a colleague, you know I can take it."

"Months? It's difficult to say. You could defy the odds. But you'll begin to sense it soon enough." He managed a smile. "Remember, rest and good food. They can work miracles."

Mary gave him a wry smile.

They shook hands.

"We'll be in touch and on top of this. That's for certain."

"I thank you again."

Her heart was crumbling but she left his office in her wheel chair with her head held high.

Eleanor watched Mary approach guided by a nurse.

"How did it go? You look white as snow."

"I'm all right. I need to stay at the hospital a few days. That's all. Just as a precaution against infection. Fortunately, he got all the cancer. Had to remove a large part of my breast. But he got it all. I feel—very fortunate."

Eleanor clasped her hands.

"I can't remember when I've been happier to hear such good news! I'd hug you so hard, but I know that would be a very bad idea."

Mary winced. "A very bad idea indeed."

"And the Alliance? Did he say how long you'll need to recuperate?"

"About a week, give or take. He's going to see me again in a few days to let me know when for sure."

"This isn't bad at all. And, of course, it goes without saying I'm not leaving. I'll do all I can to help you out. You surely know that. Along with Nora and Brigitte especially."

"And don't forget Dr. Kirov. He'll always be on call to help you."

She was quite certain she would not forget about Aaron Kirov.

The week Mary was recuperating went by. Eleanor had never been so busy and spent much time speaking with Mary and Kirov on the phone, getting their advice as needed. Mary said she requested a doctor from St. Joseph's step in full time for that week, but they were just too shorthanded. As it turned out, Kirov visited each night as well as after his rounds at St. Joseph's to advise them any way he was needed. And he surely was needed. He had to come in during the day a few times that week, once when a mill worker's son broke his arm and another time when one of the workers slid on the neatsfoot oil on the floor of the mill and broke his leg. Kirov never failed her, and she was glad he always approached her in such a businesslike manner. Her mind could not afford the complication of her emotional feelings for him at this time when she was overwhelmed by Mary's illness and work at the Alliance.

Mary did not return in a week. She said she felt such pain in the area where much of her breast had been removed and an overwhelming weakness that caused her to tell Eleanor she needed another week to recover. Of course, Eleanor understood.

But then, after four weeks and she was still unable to return and seemed weaker each time Eleanor visited she became concerned.

Surely Mary would not have lied to her. But then again…

"I don't understand it," she said to Kirov one night after she finished giving Brigitte, the night nurse, instructions before she left and Kirov finished his rounds.

"Why isn't Mary back yet? She said Dr. Birnbaum said she was fine and would be back in no time."

Kirov's eyes widened. "She told you that?" He was silent a few moments. "Eleanor, why don't we go for that cup of tea together tonight?"

She sighed. "I could use a cup."

Kirov had not so much as touched her since that day in the hospital. She felt she could surely trust him if they were merely to have a cup of tea together.

And herself.

The tea shop on Market Street lifted her heart to be removed from all the illness at the Alliance, even for a while. Small milk glass vases filled with fresh flowers sat upon Irish crocheted tablecloths. The waitress brought their tea in a Nippon china pot and cups and saucers adorned with roses.

She had stopped here often with Charles during their early marriage. Sometime he would surprise her when he came home later from the mill and bring her some of her favorite pastries, cookies or tea cakes. They would sit enjoying them in the large living room of their home on Silk Road, then in spring and summer walk the path of their magnificent garden, the wisteria hanging above them as they walked, the roses adorning each side of the path, the hydrangeas in huge globes of pink color, so many others. They never tired of discussing the garden, examining it. It was their common bond. That seemed so long ago now.

Kirov poured their tea. He spoke of his youth in Russia, then Austria. Then when he came to visit America in 1908 he heard Freud speak, along with Carl Jung and met Sandor Forenczi, another visiting analyst as well. They had been invited by Stanley Hall, the president of Clark University, to give a series of lectures on psychoanalysis. Hearing them speak changed his life. He went back to the university, learned as much as he could about psychoanalysis, met them, and they became very close. He was assigned a mentor, controversial at the time, but he learned more than he could ever have imagined.

He became excited about America with its beginning interest in the field of psychiatry and he dreamed he could be on the forefront of these beginnings. He decided he and his wife, who was against the move, would come to America permanently. Having graduated with highest honors he could easily obtain a position. But its concept was so new here. Positions were scarce And so he wound up at St. Joseph's, grateful for their openmindedness in giving him the leeway to use his abilities as an analyst at the hospital in conjunction with traditional therapy.

He poured another cup of tea for Eleanor.

"But I am talking too much about myself. Tell me about you."

She described her childhood in the tenements, her alleged father's death, her leaving school to take a position at Lafferty's Silk Mill, her work there as a ribbon weaver, the Great Silk Strike of 1913 when the workers nearly starved, Mary's encouraging her to work at the Alliance. She related the responsibility she felt for the murder of her mother, the death of her child, her estrangement from Charles a time. And how work at the Alliance saved her. She and Charles reunited after she'd nursed him back from the flu.

He was so easy to talk to. Before she knew it, she began to tell him about the darkest parts of her childhood and the sexual abuse she had suffered since she was five years old. And then when she met Dante Ravelli with his beautiful idealism she felt she could be happy with him and so she had left Charles.

"But Dante chose his idealistic causes over me. I never realized my child was so sick or I never would have left him." She squeezed her brow. "I've lived with such guilt and confusion over so many other things."

Suddenly she began to cry.

"You mustn't cry. You've had a terrible time of it, but you can be helped. I'm sure of it. These horrors can be examined and you can be set free of them. But you must trust me."

"I feel terrible now, to add to your burden but, you know," he offered, "I had an ulterior motive asking you to come with me for a cup of tea. I wish I could wait to tell you this now that I've heard what you've told me, but time is of the essence." He swirled the spoon in the hot liquid. "I think, and I hope I am right, that it would be better to hear this from me, as a doctor, as well as, I hope, a friend." He paused, continued. "You know, doctors never seem to be thought of as getting sick," he said softly. "But they can be. Dangerously so."

Her heart began to pound. He was ill. What else could it be? Her gut contracted and told her how desperately she loved him at that moment when he might be seriously ill. She would lose him. Loss bombarded her heart. Her breath came quickly. She was glad to try to sip the hot tea from the second pot they had half drunk, though her hand trembled. Something to do. Anything but face what he was going to tell her.

"You aren't well," she managed.

"Not well? No. I'm fine."

She sighed, then smiled.

"It's—Mary."

"Mary? But that can't be true. She told me Dr. Birnbaum said she was fine. I—"

He clasped her hand. "She lied to you, I'm sure, not to have you worry. But you need to know. Especially now. Because—she is not well at all. She is even worse than expected at this stage of her—cancer. I've followed the case carefully with Dr. Birnbaum. Eleanor, you must steel yourself. You must be prepared."

"But there must be something—"

"There is—nothing. Not even the hospitals in New York have any idea how to stop these cancers. And Mary let it go so long."

She half heard Kirov as he continued.

"You have a lot to think about. You must be strong when you visit her. She loves you too much to bear seeing the sorrow you feel." He sighed. "Then there's the Alliance. If Mary—won't be back—I feel it may fall upon you. Although I have no idea of Mary's wishes. But you must think about these things. And I must say," he hesitated, "you should visit

Mary as much as you can. She—loves you—so much and you are her greatest comfort. She has less time than you may think. I know I could lie to you about these things, but you would not want that, I know."

"Of course I want the truth."

She squeezed her hands around her forehead. "How will I ever get through this? How? And then there's Charles"

"I'll help you all I can. You know that."

They soon left the tea shop. Eleanor and he hardly spoke. He placed his arm around her and she did not resist. This would be the first of many times they met there, Kirov always kind and understanding, always attempting to gain her trust.

Later, they would often stand together on the Broadway bridge staring at the Passaic River, the eternal river. Its rippling and sighing sound comforted her, as it always did. She could see the tenement where she had lived in the distance. And across the river from their former apartment lay the mills, looms clacking. She thought how her life had been so intertwined with the mills, the center of her universe for such a long time. Before her work at the Women's Alliance, they supplied the pay check which fed her and her mother when she worked as a ribbon weaver.

Suddenly she felt such gladness Charles had sold the mill. They were free. Free from all its responsibility and the strikes that enveloped Paterson for years. Free from her having to live the facade of being a mill owner's wife with all the obligations it entailed. She knew now her life lay in caring for others.

But the Alliance without Mary...

She must not think of it. All her energy must be concentrated on the moment and as much as possible on Mary's comfort and happiness in the time she had left.

"I'm glad you told me." She turned to face him, saw the sadness he felt for her in his eyes. "I'm glad it was you who told me."

"I'll walk you home."

"No need."

Charles might wonder at them if he saw them together.

He read her mind. "Of course. At least let me walk you to your corner in this coming darkness, and I'll watch you go in your door."

She kissed him on the cheek. In an instant she knew she should not have. And then they were in each others' arms. She felt no fear or shame she might be seem. That unnerved her for she knew then how much she loved him.

He must have sensed his foolishness at his response where people passed by constantly.

"I can hardly bear it, waiting for emergencies, you know," he half smiled. "Just to see you at the Alliance."

"It's wrong. You have a wife, though you never speak of her. And I have an obligation to Charles, a good, kind man. This must not continue." She clenched her hands. "And now I am overwhelmed by Mary's illness. We can not—"

A dark look crossed his face. "You must understand. I love my wife. I will never say to you that I do not. But there are circumstances—"

"What circumstances? Why are you so secretive about her?"

"Isn't what I've just said to you enough for you? Believe me, I am torn with guilt over my feelings for you and the thought of my wife."

"Don't you think I feel the same way about Charles? And he needs me so."

"We must end this. The guilt we both feel will devour us." He laughed. "That certainly sounded like a comment a psychoanalyst would make. But we truly must end this. I—"

She clasped the rail of the bridge as he spoke. "But I don't know if I have the strength." She turned towards Broadway. "Walk me to my corner, will you?"

They walked to her corner in silence.

He said goodnight and left, his shoulders hunched as he walked. She watched him disappear into the evening and felt such desire for him she could barely catch her breath.

Eleanor plodded along much of the time at work in a crucible of sorrow, fearful she would wind up at a breaking point between her heartache over Mary, her worry over Charles and her desire for Kirov. A major concern now was also how Charles would bear the gravity of knowledge of his sister's death.

But one bright light shined for her in all its splendor.

On an abnormally cold day in November with sparrows hovering over a slate sky she and Charles met her father at the dock when he arrived from Ireland. She broke down in tears in his arms not only at her total joy upon seeing him but also because she felt she had a confidante whose love for her was unconditional. His would be the shoulder to lean on. She believed that and it gave her great comfort.

"Now what kinda greetin' is that? Cryin' your eyes out at the sight of your father? Do I look that bad?"

She laughed in spite of herself. "Of course not. I've never been so glad to see anyone. You must know that."

In truth, she noticed he had changed since she had seen him. He had lost weight and his clothes hung on him. That, of course, would be remedied by her cooking. But how could she remedy his graying hair, the deep wrinkles around his eyes, the light gone out of them when she studied him carefully, even though he showed such bravado. What had Ireland done to him?

Charles took care of the baggage while the two of them walked to the Pierce-Arrow.

"The trip was awful. Wore me out. I must look a sight for sore eyes."

"You need a good meal. I'll fix you up. Remember? That's my specialty now. Nursing. Not the mills anymore. Not for Charles either. You do look exhausted, I must say."

They rode home in Charles' Pierce-Arrow sharing memories of their past together. The Great Silk Strike of 1913 they had barely survived, Charles taking over the mill when his father died, his encouragement of commission weaving where workers could share in the mill owner's profits. No one mentioned the negative events, though they certainly had a shared history.

Dinner was dominated that evening by their sharing events of the day, Colin updated them on his main interest, politics. For once she was glad. She transcended her own problems, did not have the strength to tell them about Mary yet, though more and more she suspected Charles knew the gravity of her illness.

She had not had the time or inclination to read about Irish political events these past months, which she usually did. She was Irish to the bone and proud of it.

"The man who came forth as leader in our dear country was Michael Collins. He almost replaced Padraic Pearse, bless his memory, in the hearts of those who want justice for our people. But I tell you, the bloodshed, the senselessness of all those deaths. Somethin's gone out of me. And, truth told, I missed you and Charles."

"But please catch us up. We've had so much happening here, and I haven't been able to follow Irish politics."

"Truth told I don't want to talk about them anymore. It's useless. I saw that over there. Such suffering. Nobody cares about how the Irish suffer." He frowned. "I tell you it's over for me now. It's been hell. I want some peace now in my old age. I want you and Charles near me. And maybe, who knows, another grandchild."

Eleanor blushed and quickly began to clear the dishes from the table. In truth, she had wanted Charles' child thinking perhaps that would cement their relationship, draw him out of himself. But it hadn't happened. Then, too, that was before she met Kirov. She lived in a strangling maze of constant conflict now.

She knew Colin's concerns about Ireland but sensed there was something else on his mind.

"I've got some—other—work to do here now, a large part of why I came back. I've turned my back on it long enough, God knows. But I'm not wantin' to talk of it now."

And too frightened he might have added.

Mary lay in her bed, thinking back of her childhood days. How even in rain sometimes Charles and their mother would go to the garden and check the seedlings as they grew.

But not Mary. She would much rather play with her dolls and analyze their medical conditions, bandaging them for having imaginary cracked heads, broken limbs, blinded eyes, so many illnesses she, as doctor, could cure. She loved playing doctor as a child, always efficient, always healing her patients, no matter how grave their illnesses.

If only that could have been so at the Alliance.

Where did the years go?

Now she lay dying…

She could not stop herself from reminiscing, thinking about her later life when the Suffrage League filled her days, remembering the march down Fifth Avenue, twenty thousand strong. They must never give up. Never.

She remembered the time she had spent in England studying medicine and finding a great comaraderie with the women who shared her beliefs, especially Christabel and Sylvia Pankhurst and Alice Paul among so many others.

She smiled when she remembered dear Alice climbing to the roof of St. Andrew's Hall in Glasgow, standing in the icy rain, trying to draw attention to their plight at a cabinet minister's meeting. Alice stayed in that spot, immovable, all night.

She wondered what ever became of Marion Dunlop, another dear friend, who sat with her during the hunger strike when they were jailed. They finally had to have their jaws opened with a metal clamp and force fed, food pumped into them by rubber tubes pushed down their throats. She wondered how her life would have turned out if she had stayed in England. It was Christabel's fault she decided to leave. She was adamant they strive for authoritarian centralization. But Mary believed with heart and soul democracy and equality were the answers. Finally, when Christabel spoke against any link between suffrage and labor, Mary left England where she started the Women's Alliance to care for the poor, mostly the mill workers.

She knew she was right. She could see it in her patients' eyes every day.

And now she lay dying The thought struck her even harder now.

How could this possibly be? She had such great plans for eventually expanding the Alliance to help even more workers. And Eleanor, her beloved Eleanor. What would be her fate?

She thought of the first day she met her, the feisty young girl who worked at the silk mill. She felt so glad she had given her the encouragement to believe she could do more with her life and offered her a position at the Women's Alliance.

And then Eleanor marrying Mary's brother, Charles. Who could be a better match than Eleanor for her adored brother? Later, she fell in love with her but that was a secret no one else would ever know.

She was not a believer. But she felt she had done a great deal for others during her days on this earth, had saved countless lives. If there was a heaven, which she came to think about more and more as she approached death, she hoped God would consider her deeds on earth.

Kirov often came to visit Mary.

"And how are you feeling?"

"How do you think I feel? I'm dying."

Her eyes misted and she took his hand.

"I'm so glad you came now. Because I know it is near—the end."

He frowned.

"Nonsense."

"Kirov, you're a doctor. You know such things." She hesitated. "I—want to talk to you about—Eleanor."

She gasped, drew as deep a breath as she could.

His face reddened.

"I know you two are deeply in love with each other. And I'm asking you to promise me," she inhaled, "to watch over her when I'm gone. She's been through hell. I don't know what she's told you."

"She's told me a great deal. The worst. I have in mind to get her into therapy. But she's overwhelmed by—too much—right now. She realizes Ann Dodge was helped, and there is a great possibility she will be too."

He gave her a sip of juice.

"I will die a happy woman knowing that. I'm so glad you told me."

"I know how much you—love her."

She stared him straight in the eyes.

"Do you, really? Nothing has ever happened, I can assure you." she said. "And Charles, my brother. If you can make her happier, although it pains me, you have my blessing."

Kirov began to weep unashamedly.

"To think you would say this to me—about your own brother."

"There is only one person I love more than Charles. And that is Eleanor." Her hands shook as she tried to place the juice glass on the tray and Kirov helped her.

"And Charles. His drinking."

Kirov's eyes widened.

"You didn't think I knew? I'm a doctor, Aaron. The signs have been there months now. Since his child died to be exact. I want you to promise me, no matter what happens between you and Eleanor, that you will get Charles help. It's an odd request, I know, since I believe Eleanor will, in the end, choose you. But I know you. You do not take your medical code of ethics lightly."

"I'm sure he will resist, but you have my word I'll do all I can to get him help." Kirov frowned, "I don't think he has hit bottom yet, but when he does I'll be there for him. I promise."

Eleanor could not stay home from the Alliance and spent her days dutifully performing her chores, living for the afternoons or evenings when she could visit Mary, her heart a lump of glue at the thought of the loss she would have to face soon.

The weather was still quite unpredictable, but she dreamed of spring and the emerging garden. These dreams sustained her. There would be the happiness of discovery in her new garden which she had never seen in summer and filled her with anticipation. Ruffles of roses would adorn it, most likely in shocking pinks and creamy whites. Faithful salvia would sprout up in purple tongues along the walk and she knew at least a hundred hostas would deck the area adjacent to the arbor in shades of light lime to emerald green, a startling contrast to the white astilbe interspersed among them. She had seen remnants of them when they bought the house but they were now dormant. Soon they would be in full splendor. She felt filled with hope at these thoughts which sustained her and anxious to see what other surprises the garden had in store.

And it came to her she would surprise Mary on this day's visit, uplift her spirits.

She entered the sick room with the shades drawn as usual. She opened them.

"Mary, I've a surprise for you."

Mary opened her eyes, looked shocked and then laughed gleefully. The sunlight shined on Eleanor's auburn hair which was now no longer down her back. She had bobbed her hair. She swirled around so Mary could see all sides of her.

"I'm sick and tired of being old fashioned like in the teens. This is the twenties, for heaven's sake. And I want to be in style. And look at my uniform. She twirled around the room in a shorter skirt, such a change from the one she had worn to her ankles for years.

"Well, what do you think?"

"I love it! You're right in style now."

"And if Brigitte and Nora and you agree I'll order three more of the newer uniforms for us. After all, women are progressing by leaps and bounds. Gertrude Ederle just became the first woman to swim the English Channel. I guess men better start accepting women's accomplishments in this day and age. And look at women's rights, how they're progressing."

"No, just order one for Brigitte and Nora. Let's face facts, my dear. I won't be here to wear it."

Eleanor's face paled, "Why, of course you will…"

"Eleanor, we must talk. Before I'm too weak to. You surely know from the doctor that I'm dying, and you must accept that fact. I want to ask you if you'll—you'll take over the Alliance when I'm gone."

Eleanor could not speak.

"I know you're not a doctor, but you'll always have—Kirov—or one to rely on from St. Joseph's."

"Mary, I could never take your place."

"Of course you can. You are the most compassionate woman I know and have such a way with the patients. Especially the children. It's as though each child is your own."

Eleanor's eyes misted.

"Oh, my dear, I'm so sorry I said that. Robbie…"

"It's all right. I understand."

"And will you say yes? Please don't do it because it's a dying woman's wish. You must promise me that. Do it because your heart tells you to."

"If you think I'm capable enough…"

Mary showed a wan smile.

"Of course I do. Or I never would have asked you."

"Yes. Yes, I will."

"Suddenly I feel so much more peaceful. As if the dream of my life to help the poor will be passed on by you, my dear."

"I just hope I'll be worthy of it."

"You will. You will."

They did not speak a time, and Mary seemed to be pondering something in her mind.

"There's something else I must tell you, and I somehow fear it."

"There's no reason for that."

Eleanor looked perplexed.

"I must tell you something else before I'm too weak to. I've thought about it such a long time. I'm in love with you. I can't pass on without you knowing how much you mean to me."

"Mary—"

"It's all right, my dear. I know you don't feel the same way. But I'm relieved I finally had the courage to tell you after all this time. It is so forbidden I know…"

"Would it be all right if we don't talk about it now? I need to think."

"Of course."

Eleanor knew immediately she did not have the same feelings for Mary as Mary did for her. After work each day she still visited her. Today the nurse had drawn the blinds and an acrid smell was in the air. A low lamplight added a soft glow to the room.

How is she today?" She studied Mary, her face emaciated, her fingers bones. The room was a cocoon of silence.

Mary blinked her eyes but did not speak, her breath low and shallow.

Mary's nurse approached her, touched her arm, whispered, "It's near the end, I'm afraid, Mrs. Lafferty. The—very end."

"Please leave us and call her brother."

"Of course."

The sour smell of death hovered in the room, its stench filling Eleanor's nostrils.

Mary began to tremble. Her teeth chattered, though the room was warm. Eleanor held her shriveled hand, cold as ice, the one that had so often held a stethoscope to the heart of hundreds of workers, a hand that administered medication so often at no charge to people whose lives she had saved, a hand that reached out to her to give her work when she left Lafferty's Silk Mill after Angus Clegg, who had tried to rape her, returned, and she had no where to turn, a hand that always helped others before herself.

"I—love you." Mary's voice was almost inaudible.

Somehow now, as Mary lay dying, Eleanor felt she needed to show a final act of love.

She removed her skirt and laid it on the chair. Then her shoes. She lifted Mary's blanket and lay down beside her, held her close. She could feel the warmth of her body permeating Mary's. "I love you too, Mary." She continued to feel the warmth of her body emanating into Mary's flesh and she stopped shivering as Eleanor held her close. Their friendship had bound them together as one, making life so joyful and at other times hardly bearable.

"Goodbye, dearest friend," she whispered. She looked at Mary's eyes. She opened them. Did she see a glint of recognition in them? And then she heard the sound she had heard so often as she nursed others who were dying, the death rattle. She no longer felt the beating of Mary's heart next to hers. And her own heart wrenched with pain knowing Mary was dead, ever remembered, more a part of her physical self than the air she breathed.

She stared at Mary, silenced forever. She touched her precious hands, hands that had administered to and saved the lives of so many, now waxen and stiffening by the minute. She mustered all her strength and covered her eyes with her eyelids.

Her sorrow lay too deep for tears.

She held her, completely depleted, a few moments longer until she heard Charles' voice at the downstairs door, and quickly put on her skirt and shoes.

He entered, his face the color of white chalk.

"She's—gone, Charles."

Tears filled his eyes. "How can we go on without her?"

"I don't know. I truly don't."

He brushed away the tears beginning to roll down his cheeks. She felt terrified at this latest blow to him. But she knew too she must go on the way Mary wanted. She would make her work at the Alliance Mary's memorial. And she would be there for Charles.

From this tragedy, a spirit of rightness bolted through her. She finally acknowledged to Mary she understood the extent of her love, though it was a forbidden love. She felt grateful, right or wrong; in that act of lying beside her and holding her she hoped she had given her the grace of a happy death.

Mary was buried in the large family plot at Holy Sepulcher Cemetery which Eleanor thought for some reason would have displeased her, but she deferred to Charles. She would have wanted a simpler burial. But, after all, she was Charles' sister and he should have final say. His father and mother were buried there, as she supposed she would be one day. The thought made her think. She must make a will to stipulate she be cremated, her ashes dispersed in a glorious garden somewhere where she would always be a part of nature in the sacredness of earth, which had been her comfort all her life.

Eleanor stood at the gravesite, her body limp as water. A few white-throated sparrows fluttered overhead, picked some berries from the trees, then disappeared into the azure sky.

There was no breeze and the trees stood in silence, seeming to know the solemnity of the occasion. Eleanor and Charles held each other's hands in shared silence. The priest spoke briefly, according to Charles' wishes, for he knew Mary was not a religious person, though a spiritual one. Hundreds of mourners attended the church service and funeral, most from the mills, workers she had administered to often at no charge if they could not pay. For Eleanor, Mary would always live in her heart, undefeated by paltry death.

After the service, the wealthier mourners entered their carriages and left while others went on foot.

When the cemetery was empty, she looked at Charles, his face white, pasty.

"Eleanor, we should go."

"I want to stay just a short time longer."

"As you wish. I'll go back with Kosinski and leave the Pierce- Arrow for you. Are you sure you don't want me to stay?"

"I'm sure."

She did not want to subject Charles to more pain, though she suspected he was sure why she wanted to remain. As soon as he was gone and the cemetery was empty, she went to her infant's grave, once again plagued by guilt.

She had chosen a simple stone with the inscription, "Our darling, Robbie. Loved always."

She covered her face with her hands.

"Are you all right?"

She knew that voice with its clipped accent anywhere.

"Aaron, what are you doing here?"

"I was very fond of Mary. I wanted to pay my respects earlier but had a hospital emergency." He paused a few moments. "I—must admit I've been so worried about you.

I know how much Mary meant to you and haven't seen you since her passing."

She tried to rise from her child's grave. She could not. He helped her, his strength a fortress against the weakness she felt, the agony of loss permeating her.

"Let's go." He took her by the arm and they walked toward the car.

He gestured at the gravesite.

"You know, I had a child. A daughter. Oh, so briefly. She lived only a few weeks."

"I'm so sorry. I never thought to ask if you had children."

"No matter. It's just that I want you to know I understand the depth of your grief. And, more importantly, you must go on and grasp what happiness you can." He frowned. "Though guilt can do terrible things to us. It can even kill. If not the body, the spirit. Believe me, I know."

"I understand that very well."

They arrived at the Pierce-Arrow.

"No, I'll walk," He spoke a little too sharply.

"Please. Let me drive you. It will be all right if we're seen together."

"Is it that obvious I don't trust myself or our being seen together?"

They drove in silence most of the time.

"The journey to nowhere," he finally said.

"For us you mean."

"Yes."

Eleanor developed such a headache she could hardly speak or focus on driving. Memories of her son, Mary's death, her fear she would not live up to her responsibilities at the Alliance, Charles slipping back to drinking after Mary's death. And above all, the hopelessness of her love for Kirov.

"Eleanor, I must ask you this question. I can't bear it. Not having you. I can't." She glanced at him, his face pale. "Think long and carefully before you answer for I fear there will be no turning back once you do. This must end. I will have to move on based upon your answer. I can't focus on my work. I live for the times I can see you. I—do you want to go with me to a bed and breakfast out of town? I know a place. Discreet and—I'm fearful of your answer but—"

"Yes, yes," she said immediately.

The bed and breakfast was in Hawthorne, far enough from Paterson, quite cozy and pleasant looking. The late winter sun made the garden there a field of bright white. Icicles dripped from the eaves of the building. She could see the drifts of snow melting at the far side of the garden as they walked the thawing earth up the path to register and obtain a room.

He ordered a blessed bottle of wine, which calmed her nerves. They did not make small talk and she was glad. She wanted him inside her so long, wanted her legs to be entangled around his strong back, wanted him to permeate her, heart and soul. She would claim him as all hers finally. And they cleaved to each other until they both felt the burst of ecstasy building, then its explosion.

Afterwards, they held each other in complete peace. The moments, so precious, ticked by on the grandfather clock standing against the wall, warning them. Soon this must end. Soon they must put on the masks that would be their outer lives far into the future.

"I don't know how this will end," she said, after a time of silence. "There's—Charles. And your wife." She half smiled. "The mystery woman." She clasped her hands. He took them into hers and kissed them.

"Please don't mention that now. The time we have together is too precious. Please. I know. I have to do some hard thinking about— certain things—myself."

"All right, Aaron. I'll trust you know what's best. I don't have the strength to fight my feelings anymore. You have to decide for us."

"I will." He kissed her cheek. "I will."

Dusk had fallen when she returned home. Charles was waiting for her in the library.

"I'm so glad to see you." He rose, held her in his arms. "I was worried. Where were you so long?"

"I—just drove and drove. For hours."

Was this what her life would be now? The always ready lie?

"You know—," he paused.

"What is it?"

"It may sound selfish, I fear."

"Charles, you haven't got a selfish bone in your body."

"It's just that, well, Mary was my sister too. And I wish you would have informed me sooner so that I could have been with her. At the end. But," he said quickly, "I understand your need to be alone with her."

"I must apologize—"

"I won't mention it again. Shall we have some dinner?"

"Yes. I'm hungry at least."

They dined, hardly speaking. She noticed Charles' trembling hands. A sense of guilt washed over her. How could she have betrayed this decent man who was suffering so and fighting his disease with all his might?

She must break off her relationship with Kirov. There was no other way. Her mind said this, but her heart said something quite different.

The next day she found the choice of what to do concerning Kirov made for her. Dr. Swenson from St. Joseph's showed up at the Alliance.

"I'll be replacing Dr. Kirov. He wants more time for his psychoanalytic studies, and with the double work at St. Joseph's and the Alliance he's requested to be relieved of his duties here."

And so the decision had been made for her.

Everything changed after Mary's death. When her will was read, she left all her savings to Charles and the Women's Alliance with a good amount that had been left her by her father to run it to Eleanor. She did not know whether to be glad or sorry, glad because it gave her life a purpose and would serve as a memorial to Mary with every case she handled. Yet, a part of her felt regret. The grueling hours at the Alliance now that she was its owner and had such great responsibility was daunting. Though, thankfully, she still had two dedicated nurses, Nora Pennington, a sour-faced woman, who had been with the Alliance a long time, and Brigitte O'Hara, a newer nurse, a woman with clear blue eyes and creamy skin, an excellent nurse, plus help from Dr. Swenson.

She threw herself into her work. Weeks passed. She began to lose more weight. On the one hand, she knew Kirov made the right decision. Their relationship could go no where. Most likely he had seen his wife and a wave of remorse and guilt pierced him as well, too powerful to ignore.

Yet, as the days passed she could not forget him, desired just to see him. What was he doing at this exact moment? Did he ever think about her? Her body ached with a constant longing for him. And then, as usual, she plunged harder into her work, helped Brigitte and Nora in their rounds as well to keep busy and not think about her life.

Charles was a blessing at this time. Mary's will had stipulated he help her monetarily in every way with the Alliance, as needed. He told her that would happen whether Mary's will demanded it or not. He set up a separate account for her and the Alliance and told her she must feel free to use it as needed. She must not worry about rent, supplies, salaries to Nora, Brigitte or Dr. Swenson when he visited. His deposits were more than generous.

Colin was also a godsend. One day he asked her if she wasn't too tired if he could speak with her that evening. She saw a dark look cross his face, and the day at the Alliance passed slowly with the memory of that look on her mind.

That evening she plopped into her chair, exhausted as usual, but tried to look cheerful.

"So, darlin', how was your day?"

"Depressing. Valentino died." He had been Eleanor's favorite male star, part of Eleanor's fantasy and the world that helped block her mind from reality. She loved the films: Charlie Chaplin, the Keystone Kops, and Douglas Fairbanks, another of her idols. She and Charles had just seen the first Hollywood cartoon to feature sound, *Steamboat Willie*.

In so many ways it was an exciting time to be alive.

"We did have only five new patients today. Two with pneumonia. The mills are not forgiving when it comes to spread of disease or illness. But we know that, don't we?"

"Truth said, I miss the mills. I'm thinkin' of goin' back."

"But—"

"What I find is I'm bored. And I still have a few good years in me. I thought I'd apply to Flanagan's mill, if they'll have me."

"Is that what you wanted to tell me?"

"Not really." He stared at his hands.

Her heart began to pump harder. What if he was sick—if—"Are you all right?"

"Well enough. Truthfully, it was hell workin' with Michael Collins. Danger all around. But I'm through with that life. Although if there's a need for a union leader once I get a job, I don't know as I'd turn it down, truth be told."

She smiled. "You'll never change. Helping the workers is in your blood, just as it was in Dante's."

"Course I never did hear from him. How could I? Over there. I don't suppose you ever—"

"No."

"It's just as well." He paused a few moments. "I need to tell you somethin'. You should of known it a long time ago. You have an aunt." "An aunt! How wonderful. But why in the world wouldn't you tell me?"

"Because, God forgive me, I was ashamed. And I hope and pray you'll forgive me for it. It's one of the reasons I came back. To make things right."

"Forgive you for it? I don't understand. Why didn't I ever meet her? It would have given me a sense of family. I would have loved—" "It isn't like that. She's in Redstone Lunatic Asylum. Has been for years. She lives in her own world. She wouldn't know you. Hasn't known me for years."

"But why did this happen to her?"

"Do you think I know what makes people lose their mind? I don't have an answer."

"But I have to see her. She's my aunt."

"I used to go see her at least once a month. But then with leavin' for Ireland she's completely alone there. Not a visitor. I just couldn't stand the thought of it. I let her down terrible. Which is a crazy thing for me to say because she doesn't even know if I'm there or not. But if she should pass on—"

"You should have told me."

"You had enough on your mind at the time. I couldn't burden you with more."

"You can't be sure she doesn't know you. The touch of your hand, your holding her in your arms. Human contact. These things may be a connection. I've been reading about mental illness a great deal. There are psychiatrists who specialize in mental problems and I've seen their methods work. Dr. Kirov, for example."

"But you don't want to go to Redstone. It's not like the hospital you imagine, not like St. Joseph's."

"Of course I'm going. Even if I have to go alone."

"I can't have you do that."

"We'll go Sunday."

Colin sighed. When Eleanor made up her mind, there was no changing it.

Redstone Lunatic Asylum stood at the top of a hill just outside of Paterson. It was a massive sandstone building that showed signs of wear. The window ledges had peeling paint but the windows were clean. A visitor to the asylum would have no complaint about the spotlessness they tried to project. The steps leading to the massive front door had pieces of stone missing here and there. She looked up to see an antique clock, ornate and shiny, which gave the wrong time.

They rang the bell. Finally, a nurse answered and invited them to enter.

The inside was not at all as Eleanor had imagined. Although the sun shined brightly, the windows were small and let in little light. Yet, she felt a sense of orderliness and cleanliness to the place. The nurse explained the basic set up of the building when they inquired. It possessed three distinct sections.

The first was for those who could function decently but were treated for nervous disorders. They each had separate rooms, were able to eat on their own as well as bathe. Many of the patients here were not on prolonged stays. In fact, many were wealthy people who stayed a short to extended time while they recuperated.

They were free to walk the floor and grounds as they wished.

The second ward was for the more deeply disturbed who often needed help with the daily routines of existence common to those who lived in society. They were not in cells but were carefully monitored and had to notify the nurse if they were leaving their rooms for any reason. Some were not well enough to eat in the dining room and their meals were brought to them.

The third ward was for those classified as severely disturbed. The nurse said they would be described by society as insane. Some had cell mates; others did not, depending on the severity of their illness. Most of these patients could not bathe themselves and had to be fed by the nurse or force fed. She said they were in various forms of therapeutic rehabilitation but did not elaborate.

Her Aunt Colleen was in Ward Three.

"Wait in Room 6," an owl-faced nurse said, pointing the direction to them.

"I don't think this was a good idea, darlin'. Not at all."

Colin began to pace back and forth.

When they arrived at Room 6, Eleanor insisted they explore what lay past the door. They opened it and went through a hallway to another room, opened its door to find there were at least twenty patients before them. They appeared either confused and pacing or catatonic. A few sat in the far corner of the room on the floor, rocking back and forth.

A nurse approached. "This is the recreation room. You shouldn't be here without an aide. You'll be called in due time."

"We'd like to see Colleen McLaughlin. Now."

She frowned, then pointed to a woman who was sitting on the floor, her back against the wall. Eleanor could see her long, gray hair in tangles, her crinkled skin, a tear in her gray uniform.

The nurse walked over to Colleen. "It's someone to see you, dear." She grasped her arm. "Now stand up, won't you?" The nurse lifted her, with Colin's help, and led her to the visitors' room down the corridor.

"You should have waited in Room 6. Didn't they tell you? Didn't you see the guard? How did you ever get past him?"

"We wanted to see the rest of your hospital. This is horrible. These are human beings."

"They're also, in many cases, dangerous. They can turn on you at the drop of a hat."

"I don't see that. I see most of them heavily medicated so they don't give you any problems."

"You don't understand, miss. We do our best. Believe me, we can hardly get nurses and aides to work here."

The visitors' room was appropriately cheerful, painted a pale yellow. A calendar on the wall showed floral scenes but the wrong month. The chairs looked as though mass produced but they were clean and comfortable enough. A frayed oriental carpet lay on the floor. A lamp with an old floral shade sat on a long oak table at the center of the room.

"Colleen, this is Eleanor, your niece."

Eleanor could hear the tremble in Colin's voice.

She scrutinized her aunt, her disheveled hair, her wide eyes, blank stare, hands shaking uncontrollably.

Colin saw the shock on Eleanor's face. "They quiet her down but don't do much else."

"Hello, Colleen. I'm glad to meet you." She shook her hand, wondered when the last time was when she felt the warmth of a human touch, fought back the tears.

"She doesn't mean it, you know. Not shakin' your hand back doesn't mean she doesn't like you or anything. She's just in her own world. It would be a miracle if she came out of it."

"Colleen, it's Eleanor. Your niece." Colleen continued to stare past her at an elusive netherland only she could penetrate.

And so Eleanor sat in silence with Colin, holding Colleen's hand. Colin had brought some fruit. He took out a peach and placed it on her mouth. She bit into it; juice ran down her chin onto her uniform. He fed her the rest of the peach; she spit the pit onto the floor.

"She does eat, thankfully. Otherwise, they'd have to force feed her, stick a tube down her throat."

They stayed a long time. How could she leave such a pitiful woman behind? She could not imagine parting.

After a time the nurse knocked, entered.

"I'm sorry. It's time for Colleen's medication. Plus it's her dinner time in a few minutes."

They walked back to the ward with the nurse who protested their doing so. But Eleanor threatened her with a lawsuit if they were not allowed to see the larger ward. She had no idea if that had any validity. But, thankfully, the nurse assumed it did.

They entered the larger ward just as the aides came in, lining the patients up. Those able to stand were led to the dining area. Colleen was to stay behind. An aide brought her to the other side of the room and began feeding her.

Eleanor surveyed the room. About fifteen or so patients incapable of feeding themselves sat or stood waiting their turn to be fed.

She noticed a beautiful, blonde-haired woman whose hair flowed down her back sitting in the corner.

Eleanor approached the nurse.

"That woman. Why isn't she moving? She appears paralyzed."

"She's just in her own world."

She approached the woman, feeling if she held her hand perhaps at least she would sense human contact.

Her face was even more beautiful close up; wrinkle free, eyes clear as green crystal, hair flowing in blonde ripples framing her heart- shaped face. She clasped the woman's hand. She did not respond but stared at Eleanor.

And then she noticed her name tag.

On it was written "Anna Kirov."

Kirov's mind was bombarded with the revelations Eleanor had made to him. He wiped the sweat from his brow. He could not help Eleanor enter that deep area of her unconscious mind, bring forth her disturbances and begin the slow process of cure for one of Freud's major tenets was that the psychoanalyst and patient were forbidden to have an emotional, let alone physical relationship. His hands seemed tied by giant ropes which would not unknot and help him to free her. He paced the floor of his small apartment on Market Street. He wished he could lie down and fall asleep. Every bone in his body ached; another migraine was slowly easing its way into his head. That would surely be the end to any rest. He filled the kettle with water and checked his supply of tea. That would sustain him most of the night. He had not made the decision to stop visiting the Alliance lightly.

Eleanor inhabited so much of his waking moments he found he must work slower so that his focus was clearer and he was less likely to make errors at the hospital. The revelations she had made to him at the tea shop were monumental. And why had she chosen this Dante Ravelli? A man dedicated to the cause of justice so strongly would always have that as his main priority. So why had she fallen in love with a probably unattainable man? She was drawn to her idealistic movie magazines with perfect stars in them. Was that part of it? He did not sense that her relationship with Charles was perfect either. How had she survived so long without breaking down? What was blocking her from having a real relationship? Why had she once again chosen a man for all intents and purposes could not give her a lasting togetherness, for Kirov was married. Had the terror from her being sexually abused as a child been so deep she avoided or disbelieved she could have one, that her experience affected her to that extent? Quite possibly.

He wondered about Charles. As kind and understanding as he was, he seemed to be deeply flawed and weak, no match for her. He wondered what her sexual relationship could be with Charles. He was kind and understanding but he seemed so flawed, no match for her. Of course, worse of all, it wasn't possible for Kirov to truly help her, to delve into her unconscious mind. Yet, his mind whirled every time he thought of their conversation that day in the tea shop. How could he help her? How could he help himself he was so madly in love with her? He wanted her to get well. He felt the depressions she was experiencing were worsening, that she must be feeling worse and worse. He stood by her at the Alliance feeling so helpless, which was also part of his leaving.

But he must think. Think. There had to be a way out of this conundrum.

So much of his other hours at home also focused on Anna and the turmoil he felt concerning both women. He had helped and cured many patients when he was in Austria with guidance from Freud, Jung and Ferenczi and had survived his internship with highest honors; yet, he could do nothing for Anna. Was he fated to live a life spent visiting her weekly and being estranged from Eleanor? How could he help her? She was so constantly depressed and leading such an unfulfilling life. And how could he help himself? The guilt he felt from loving Eleanor gnawed at him constantly as he felt he betrayed Anna. Which was foolish. Did she even know he existed?

He had met her by chance. One of his patients had been unable to make his appointment and Anna Zolov, his daughter, stopped by to tell him he had the flu, which had such an immediate onset it was too late to call to cancel the appointment. She came to pay him for the missed time but he refused. From the instant he saw her he was smitten. She seemed genuinely interested in his work. He asked her if she would like to have lunch sometime and she agreed.

He was once again struck by her beauty when she entered the restaurant where they agreed to meet. Her eyes were the color of sea glass and her face possessed a natural glow. She had worn her flaxen-colored hair in a demure chignon which coiled thickly at the nape of her neck. Her dress was of a fine green watered silk which complimented her eyes.

She spoke of her childhood in Vienna. Even from an early age, her father exposed her to the culture and museums that surrounded them. As she grew older, he took her to specific galleries. She had fallen in love with the work of the artist Gustav Klimt and she had urged her father to purchase his works. This indicated to Kirov she came from a very cultured background. She also spoke of her great love of her father and mother, although she hated their sheltering her so, even in adulthood. This meeting, she admitted, was one her parents knew nothing of. They had a pleasant lunch, though she merely picked at her chicken and salad and he noticed her hands trembled.

Her father and mother, both somewhat unwell, disapproved of their marriage. They were suspicious of this strange, new field, psychoanalysis. Could Kirov make a living at it? But Anna loved him. She defied them and married him quietly in Vienna. To add to her parents' heartbreak he told her he wanted to go to America and be on the forefront of this burgeoning field. And so this shy, introverted, frightened girl agreed to go to America to start a new life with him, leaving all that was familiar to her. She had seemed accepting at first, but only later did he realize the damage her leaving her family, home, and friends would cause.

In America he became involved with the psychoanalytic movement that was emerging. But he felt great conflict in the group. Freud believed that men should be trained by mentors and he defended that position staunchly. What Kirov learned from his mentor in Vienna helped him immeasurably. However, the society in America largely rejected the emphasis upon mentoring and felt each psychoanalyst must learn from his own victories and failures.

He soon broke away from the group, lost in a miasma of confusion until a friend from the group mentioned he learned St. Joseph's in Paterson was in need of a medical doctor but felt certain the open-minded Dr. Belli, might be willing to allow him to use his psychoanalytic skills as needed. The relationship worked out. After Dr. Belli died, he worked for Dr. Birnbaum who was impressed by Kirov's successes.

These successes helped him alleviate the pain he felt at his wife's unhappiness in America.

Anna's adjustment to the United States was difficult from the beginning. She spoke no English and did not seem interested in learning. She sat pining away for home and family. She and Kirov, however, were happily in love. Since he still needed to save to get his own practice started and support them, he was glad to take the position at St. Joseph's.

Then Anna miscarried. A month later they received word her parents were dead. Her father had taken the life of her mother who had been unwell for years and then committed suicide.

That was when the horror started. She began to live in her own world, stare into space for hours, refused to eat. He used every medical and psychoanalytic skill he possessed to try to reach her. He consulted with the best doctors in New York City. Their answer was the same.

Redstone Lunatic Asylum.

And so his beloved Anna lived in a state of death in life, as he often felt he did each day.

Until he met Eleanor. His decision not to see her again must be final. Yet, she needed help he could not give because of their relationship. He felt like one of the mice he experimented with in his student days, trapped in mazes and cages. He managed to go through the outward signs of normalcy. Yet, he felt the guilt he would have known if he continued to betray Anna would have been more unbearable.

Colin noticed a great difference in Eleanor these past weeks. He thought he discovered the reason when he visited what had been Charles' silk mill and was now Flanagan's.

He stood in shock when he entered his former job site. Charles had told him the IWW had lost much ground in Paterson because of the workers' disgust at their constant in-fighting which did nothing to further their cause of better working conditions and wages. The Jewish Workmen's Circle was truly the most broken away. The broad silk weavers were now printing their own books, sponsoring their own school and hospital, supporting a singing society and orchestra and becoming even more bitter rivals to the IWW with its large Italian membership.

Colin liked the ideas of the Brotherhood of American Silk Workers, the BASW, who tried to create more tolerance between capital and labor but then heard the workers were mistrustful the group was really on the side of the silk manufacturers.

The United Textile Workers emerged as well and claimed to have enrolled most of the city's ribbon weavers. Charles said he heard over fifteen hundred broad silk weavers had joined.

"Colin!"

He was taken aback by Stephen Kosinski. "My friend, I heard you were back in Paterson. And to weaving, I hope. We can use you. But it's all different now. As you can see."

He led him to the area where previously the giant silk looms clacked away, the weavers creating magnificent floral silks that would adorn the wives of the mill owners, along with other wealthy women, and drapes, hats, and ribbons.

"So what do you think, compared to what used to be this floor?"

Colin looked around and saw most of the area was cramped and divided into what must be commission weaving machine areas. It had been expanded into a broad silk mill. They had grown a great deal during the war and now he said there were close to two hundred broad silk workers.

Colin's stomach churned. This was a broad silk mill now. Most were Jewish owned, causing great conflict.

"A lot of the Jews, now they want to open their own small shops and move from being working class. Can't say I blame them. But now some of them, they buy up a mill and some of their own families work in the shops, their own people. It's a real problem. A lot of Jews are outraged by it."

"Can't say I blame 'em." Colin punched the air. "Don't they realize yet how important unity is—the Jews, Italians, Greeks, Poles—we have to be united or we'll get nowhere fast. That was what the IWW tried to preach."

"You sound like your old self. And just the man we need right now."

Colin hesitated, "I'm pretty much finished with that," he said finally. "Someday I'll tell you about—Ireland."

"We need you. The ASW is the key union in Paterson now. They are for local rule and democratic control. Mostly it's the ribbon weavers. But the manufacturers. They have their own agenda."

"It sounds a total mess to me. And I do smell another strike in the air."

"There's talk of one. Some say it's mostly from the ASW. They say a lot of Commies have infiltrated the unions while you've got your ASW leaders of mostly German and English descent. Personally, I don't think it's fair not one important leader of the ASW's a Jew."

"I know one thing. I need work. Period. I need money bad. I can't live off Eleanor and Charles. And right now I don't want to be involved with unions. I just don't have the strength to—after Ireland." His eyes misted. "It was hell over there."

Kosinski placed his hand on Colin's shoulder. "I understand. And you can probably start here anytime. With your skills. I'll set you up with a loom, explain commission weaving and your profit. I guess there must be so much tension in the house with Charles' drinking problem and all, and this place will be a refuge for you. Poor Eleanor. I don't know how she—"

"Drinking problem? Charles?"

Kosinski's face paled. "God, now I've put my foot in my mouth."

"Tell me. Everything. I had no idea—" Colin clenched his arm. "I have to know. For Eleanor's sake as well as his."

"It got bad, oh, over a year ago. He drank a lot before Eleanor found out. He promised her he'd stop he told me. As far as she thinks, he has. But he hasn't. Not a bit. He's worse than ever, truth be told. He must of just got smarter in hiding it."

Colin scratched his head. "How could I be so dumb I didn't notice?"

"I know where he gets it from. And believe me, he hasn't stopped. Worse than ever. The man needs help." Kosinski hesitated. "And— I'm sorry to say I wasn't far behind him. But my wife. The kids. I made up my mind to beat it. And I'm really tryin'. And doin' good. So far, at least."

"I give you credit."

Colin understood now. Eleanor so withdrawn. Charles' drinking must have preyed upon her, not knowing where to turn, not wanting to involve him.

Well, he knew now. She would not suffer any longer if he had his say. And he knew exactly what he would do about it.

Eleanor sat, thin as breath, sipping tea when Colin came down for breakfast. Within her parched throat her anguish felt relief a time with her blessed radio on playing "Can't Help Lovin' That Man of Mine" from *Show Boat*. What would she do without her blessed radio? They would gather around it every night; the thrill of people speaking and singing to them never ceased. She tried with all her strength to listen to it. Her head felt as though it weighed a hundred pounds.

"Eleanor, I'm worried about you. These severe depressions you have. You've had them for years. You need help." Colin suggested.

"I'm all right."

Truthfully her head felt as though it weighed like lead. She did her best not to show it but it was harder and harder to disguise her severe depression.

Every time Charles went out Eleanor searched the house thoroughly and found no liquor. At least she had that to be grateful for.

As for Kirov, she ached to the bone to see him once more, even if just passing on the street, even if he did not acknowledge her. She still felt the shock from seeing Anna Kirov at the asylum and could imagine what guilt he was feeling over their love.

Colin scrutinized her plate. "That doesn't seem much of a breakfast. How about some toast and cereal with that tea?"

"I ate so much last night I feel uncomfortable eating more."

He frowned. "I'm worried about you not eating."

Eleanor blushed.

"I ate later again. More chicken, mashed potatoes, carrots. And a big piece of apple pie." She pretended a smile.

"I don't know who you're tryin' to fool." He went to the ice box, opened it. "There's all the food left from last night. Plus two pieces of pie gone. One I ate and one Charles ate last night."

She stared at the tablecloth, did not respond."

I went to Flanagan's yesterday."

"Really?" "Everything's changed. But I'm startin' Monday to commission weave. Might as well give it a try. I just can't sit around and twiddle my thumbs anymore."

Eleanor sipped her tea slowly.

"Why didn't you tell me about Charles' problem with drink? Why wouldn't you share such a burden now that I'm here? I'm your father. I want to help you. Always."

She almost choked on her tea. "What are you talking about? He did have a problem, I admit. But it's over. He promised me."

He got up from the table and put his arms around her.

"You have to face the facts about Charles. You'll have a problem with him for the rest of his life, I believe. Life with him is goin' to be hard. It's somethin' he can't control, though God knows, he tries for himself, and for you. Why didn't you tell me he's still drinkin' worse than ever? I got the information from a good source. I hate to tell you, believe me, but we've got to get him help. No doubt about it."

They sat quietly a time.

"You don't understand. When Charles is out, if the truth be told, I search all the possible places he could be hiding it. As tired as I am, I do it. Nothing."

"Kosinski told me he's drinkin' heavily again," he said slowly. "That he has sources of getting it."

"But he hardly goes out at night. Not that much. And he's excited about starting courses in landscape architecture. He got the bulletin in the mail. Well, it was a few months ago. He hasn't applied yet. He's involved with plans for the garden again. He wants to enlarge the area in the back and create a memorial garden for Robbie. So you see, you and Kosinski are wrong. Why, he spends most of his time in the greenhouses. Planning and—"

Panic shot through her. Then numbness. The room began to sway. She quickly sat down on the chair.

She knew Colin had the same thought she did. He sat down across from her, took her hand in his. "Breathe deep."

Eleanor felt frozen in place. She literally could not move. Then a wave of dizziness threatened to overcome her.

She envisioned all the years ahead of her with Charles. There would be times he would be sober and everything would be wonderful for them; the garden would satisfy his need for a touch of beauty in a life that for him was dark and frightening at times.

And what would her life be like? She would spend her life on pins and needles worrying each day if that would be the one he decided he desperately needed a drink. And would he be willing to go for rehabilitation? And if he did, would it work?

And Kirov. What of him? She would see him now and then on the days he was at the Women's Alliance and think of what might have been…

Colin shook her hard.

"Breathe deep, I said."

She did as he asked. After a time, the wave of dizziness subsided. "I'm all right."

They donned their raincoats and galoshes, for a heavy rain was pounding the earth and house. But this could not wait.

In appearance the greenhouse looked fine. Charles' picotees and other rare specimens looked quite healthy. He had been working on them, she could see. She felt hope. But the seed pots and larger ones remained empty of plants, untouched. By now he and their gardener should surely have accomplished more than this if they'd both been working.

She did see rows of seedlings across the aisle which Tom, their gardener, might have started.

They looked around, knowing what they must do. The giant pile of soil in its wooden container in the corner was the first spot they chose.

"We'll work from the back of the greenhouse to the front," Colin suggested. "You know I can do this myself. Why don't you go inside and—"

"I have to know."

They plunged their hands, arms into the bin and pulled out six bottles of gin, all full. They checked thoroughly and carefully the soil in some of the giant pots.

He faced her once they got in the house, soaked. "Don't tell him we know. Not yet. I have a plan and it wouldn't be good if he knew we know. And don't you think for a minute this isn't breakin' his heart. What he knows it would do to you if you found out. The hell he's goin' through."

She blew her nose in her handkerchief.

"Thankfully you have the Alliance. Work to occupy your mind. Those people need you."

She tried to do what Colin suggested and threw herself back into work. Yet, though she had lived through so much upheaval in her life and tried to face it with courage, she felt a fear permeating her, a fear she would break down. And she must not. Charles was an inebriate. He needed her. She must rise to the occasion and help him as best she could. He was too good a man to let him fight his demons alone. Kirov would be the first to agree. That was why she loved him so.

Ida Dratch, whose face reminded one of a sour lemon, had a few more minutes of duty as a nurse at St. Joseph's Hospital when Colin entered.

"Could I speak with a doctor?"

"Is it an emergency?"

"Well, yes and no."

"Why don't you come back tomorrow if it's not that serious?"

"But I want to speak with somebody now."

A man across the way with his back to him caught his eye. He looked so much like Dante Ravelli; same build, hair length. Until he turned.

"Perhaps I can help you. Why don't you follow me down the corridor? I have an office there." He extended his hand. "I'm Dr. Kirov."

When they reached his office Colin closed the door.

"And what seems to be troubling you, Mr?"

"McCarthy. Colin McCarthy. It isn't me. It's my son-in-law. He needs help. Alcohol. It's taken him over. He's a very well known man in Paterson, and I don't know what he'd do if he was found out. The shame. His wife, my daughter, has been hurt just as bad. He lied to her, told her he was off the stuff. But by her looks I know somethin's wrong. I think maybe she just didn't want to face it. She hardly eats. Thin as a rail. Is there a medicine you could give me for him, to help him out? Though I fear he needs more than that, needs to be sent away a time. God knows, I hope not."

"If only there was a medicine. I'm convinced this is a disease, this alcohol addiction, but my colleagues disagree. Yet, what man in his right mind would do this to himself unless he was powerless, unless his body craving was greater than his heart and soul?"

"What should I do?"

"I'm so glad you came. Hopefully, he may be ready to finally accept treatment. There's a place I know. Willow Haven, in Minneapolis, that treats inebriate illness, as it's called. That is a sad commentary, so few places exist, when so many men and women need help. Of course, some of the local mental hospitals have separate wards for such illnesses but in most cases are inadequate."

"I can't just twiddle my thumbs while my son-in-law falls lower and lower. And my daughter. She's my life. Thankfully, her job at the Women's Alliance keeps her mind somewhat occupied, but now she's found he deceived her—"

"The Alliance on Market Street? I worked there a while. Is your daughter's name Eleanor?"

"Yes, but—"

"Please don't worry. What we say here is in strict confidence. I would never breathe a word of this conversation to anyone. But will you promise me to do the same? I don't think you should tell your daughter you spoke with me. It might—upset her more. Her standing, and her husband's in the community. Plus her fears for him. I will investigate a place he can go. Do you agree?"

"I do."

He wrote down the name of the hospital in Minneapolis and gave it to Colin. "You can call and get information. And in the meantime, I'll search for other places."

"Minneapolis. It's too far. If you could check for other places nearer—"

"Of course."

Kirov stood, shook Colin's hand. "I give you all the credit in the world trying to help him."

"It's for my daughter's sake as much as his. I love her more than my own life."

And so do I, Kirov thought. And so do I.

Charles consented to go to Mountain Grove Hospital for Dipsomania and Inebriates, as it was named, for "the cure."

Although Redstone Asylum had a facility, it seemed better to send him to Mountain Grove in upstate New York. He would be far enough from Paterson no one would find out but not as far as Minneapolis. He and Eleanor would say he was on a business trip for a new venture he had in mind. She put on her best acting skills when he was admitted, but Colin sensed something was dreadfully wrong when they got home.

She had hardly spoken on the way back and had always so enjoyed the chance to drive the Pierce-Arrow.

When they arrived home, she went up to her room, bathed, turned the radio on. They were playing a jaunty tune from *No, No Nanette,* but it didn't help. She lay there with the slightest hope Charles would improve.

Colin came home from the mill exhausted each day for commission weaving was hard work if one wanted a profit. Unfortunately, he never failed to bring back down the meal Eleanor rejected when the cook brought it upstairs. He considered it a victory nowadays if she drank some broth.

"I don't understand this, darlin'. Charles is in good hands. He'll come through. You know how much he worships the ground you walk on. I'm guessin' you told him to shape up for once and for all. And he will. I know it. So please get back to your old self again."

If only she could tell him she was in constant agony over her loyalty to Charles and her love for Kirov. She forced herself to get to the Alliance each day and found some respite there. Was this what love always brought? Pain? Suffering? She twisted her fingers which were like sticks. She felt the dark, heavy cloud of depression seizing her. Its hands squeezed her brain. She wanted to be well but she could not help herself. She tried to read the latest *Photoplay* with Greta Garbo, her favorite female star of the twenties, on the cover. It was useless. She finally succumbed to her mood and lay in a fetal position on the bed, convinced no one could help her, though she thought of Kirov and his comments that he could…

She lay half asleep, the drapes half drawn. Better to be enveloped in semidarkness. She tried to fight the depression that had set in. She must find strength to get out of bed, to get to the Alliance the next day. Yet, the task seemed insurmountable. She was in the grip of a miasma of sadness beyond her control. Charles' face haunted her, and that of Anna Kirov. Their lives were at a dead end. She and Kirov could never find happiness together.

She knew the knock on the door was her father's.

He entered and went to fully open the drapes.

No. Leave them that way."

He frowned. "This can't go on. Not only do you not eat, but you're so blue. You need help. You must believe Charles will be all right and stop worrying about him."

"Let me be. Please. I'll come out of this. I need time."

"Well, I think I may have a partial answer."

In a few moments there was another knock at the door.

"Please. Let me be."

The door opened. Colin left. Then a figure walked across the room.

"Eleanor. Your father called me. I hope you don't mind. He's so worried about you."

Kirov. She would have known his voice anywhere. She noticed he had lost much weight.

He sat down on the bed, lifted her limp body into his arms. "Your father has no idea of our relationship. He called me for help. My dear, we can not be separated again. I can't bear it. And I see by your state, neither can you. You are in too much turmoil over Charles. Over me. And I see such a pall hangs over you. I believe it goes back to events of your childhood especially, your formative years. You must get help."

She felt infused with life as he held her, once again becoming a breathing, living being. His warm body comforted her.

"What can we do?"

"Be together. As much as we can. I love you, Eleanor. I can no longer fight my feelings. We are too involved for me to treat you but I know someone, Nathan Brodsky, who I believe can help you. He studied with Fritz Neuhauer, a leading Viennese disciple of Freudian psychiatry. You must promise me you will think about getting his help. You don't have to answer immediately". He hesitated. "But very soon."

She turned her head away. "But—"

"Please. Please. Trust me. Eleanor, don't spoil it. Let us hold onto what we have. I can not let you go."

"All right. You must decide for us."

"I will. First," he smiled, "you must eat. Will you do that for me?"

"I'll try. Yes. Yes."

"And get stronger each day? I'll come to see you."

"My father?"

"I told you. He only knows me as a doctor. He came to St. Joseph's looking for a doctor for Charles. And now for you. I happened to be there," he smiled. "Destiny. You see? It's on our side."

"I'm not sure I believe that. But you're here."

"Your father need not know about us."

"I agree."

He lay her back on the bed. "My God, you are so weak. But we'll fix that. You must eat. And I will see about getting you help."

He rose, called Colin. "Bring her some food immediately. And include a big bowl of hearty soup if you have it."

Colin and he watched her eat her soup, chicken, potatoes, string beans, dessert.

Colin squeezed his chin. "Doctor, you are a miracle worker."

"I'll be back tomorrow evening after my hospital rounds, Mrs. Lafferty. And I hope your father will report you've had a good breakfast and lunch."

Colin and Kirov paused at the door.

"Whatever did you do or say to make her feel so much better? I'm in your debt for life."

"I assured her that—her husband would improve. Among other things."

"But I've told her that so many times and it didn't help. It must be because you're a doctor. You're a miracle worker."

A miracle worker. Kirov smiled all the way home.

Kirov was true to his promise and spoke with Dr. Brodsky about working with Eleanor. Kirov visited Eleanor nightly. Colin felt he could have come fewer times as Eleanor improved but did not question it. After two weeks she was back on her feet again and returned to the Alliance.

She met Kirov once a week at the bed and breakfast in Hawthorne where they had come the first time they were intimate, both living for that one day each week. He was a wonderful lover. Patient. Kind. Passionate. She never thought she could love someone as completely as she had loved Dante Ravelli. But Dante's idealism was his first love. She was Kirov's. He was completely hers. His love for her, his compassion for his patients and her, his intellectuality, his idealism, drew her to him like a flame to dry wood.

The weeks passed and they were lost in the bliss of their moments together, blocking out all responsibility to others, except to themselves and their unrelenting love, refusing to think of its consequences.

Kirov waited and waited for her to speak of seeing Dr.

Brodsky but she said nothing. He could only hope she was seriously weighing its merits.

One day when they met, Kirov became strangely quiet.

"What is it?"

"I must tell you about—my wife."

Should she tell him she knew? It would perhaps be best if he told her and unburdened himself. And if he realized she knew he would guess her deep depression and illness had also risen not only from guilt and conflict over Charles and him but also over the tragedy of the broken life she saw in Anna that day at the asylum. What it took from him to live with the guilt of betraying such a delicate creature and from her having such knowledge was transcended to an extent by their need to be together. But could their love last through such an agonizing situation?

"I have to tell you the truth. Everything. I can no longer live with deceit." He grasped his knees. "My wife—"

"I should have told you long ago." She hesitated. "Your wife, Anna. I know. It was part of why I couldn't function. Knowing I would not only be betraying Charles. But seeing her face before me I realized what you must be going through."

"Good God! How did you know?"

"I visited my aunt at Redstone Asylum. Colin never told me about her. When I was there I saw this woman. Alone. So beautiful. I approached her to try to comfort her. And then I saw her name tag."

He began to pace the room.

"Does anyone else know?"

"Of course not."

"That has been the plague of my existence. That with all my knowledge of psychiatry I can do nothing—nothing—to help her." He turned to her. "And how do you feel now?"

"That day, when you came to my room, when I heard you say my name, I knew I would love you until the day I die."

"Perhaps we do deserve some happiness. As long as Anna and Charles are not hurt. No matter what, they must never be hurt."

And so their pact was made They lay on the bed and held each other a long time, at peace. They had shared their secrets and would never let each other go.

And they believed it.

Charles was at the Mountain Grove Hospital for Dipsomania and Inebriates in Massachusetts during this time. Kirov recommended it because it followed the Emmanuel Movement, founded by a clergyman, Dr. Elwood Worcester, who had success with many patients and used a more psychiatric approach.

The movement was an attempt to treat a variety of neurotic disorders. It was based on the premise that all diseases, including dipsomania, which he treated as a disease, had spiritual as well as mental composition. Each day Charles was subjected to one of the main tenets of the protocol, relaxation therapy and suggestion, including autosuggestion, to reach the unconscious mind. Worcester believed dipsomaniacs could be improved by redirecting their attention away from their problems to a life of service and spirituality.

Charles was interested in this approach, thinking perhaps if he came outside of himself more he could be helped. It certainly worked with Eleanor at the Alliance. And he readily became involved in prayer and group support. He worked hard at self-improvement. The therapy sessions, designed to reduce patients' guilt felt as a result of being slaves to alcohol and rejection by family and society, rather than preaching temperance, were strong motivators for him. His mentor explained that his recovery must come from surrender to outside helpful forces as well as the unconscious, for it was important to remember alcohol, not one's life history, caused alcoholism, that it resulted from physical and mental tension, which Charles certainly understood.

Relaxation therapy did seem to be helping him. He also learned the importance of detailed time plans so he would use his time constructively and was instructed in methods of controlling his feelings, especially anger, whether expressed or unexpressed. Learning to relax was a key to cure. He had a radio in his room and enjoyed listening to baseball games, especially admiring Babe Ruth, Red Grange, and Knute Rockne. They even let him stay up later to watch the Dempsey vs. Tunney fight.

Charles worked even harder to improve. He listened attentively to his mentor's suggestions and took copious notes. He must conquer this demon. Not only his life but his life with Eleanor depended upon it.

Kirov continued to visit his wife. She had become even more wan and withdrawn with each therapy they tried. On his last visit he was taken aback by her appearance. Her teeth had been removed, which he knew was based on one of the theories of the day of John Cotton. It was thought that it was a way of releasing impurities from the body which congested one and caused mental illness. But still, thin and weak, her large, glassy eyes seemed as blank as ever. He held her cold hands, rubbed them.

"Anna, my darling. I have helped many others. Why can't I help you? Speak to me. Please. Just one word. Let me know you recognize me at least. I'm here to tell you something. That you will always have a place in my heart. Always. That I am still reading and reading and corresponding with psychiatrists in Vienna about cases like yours and trying to understand, to help you. Do you hear me? I will never abandon you. Never." He hesitated. "Even if I met—someone else. Is that clear? Do you hear me, Anna? Squeeze my hand if you do, if you don't want to speak."

Her hand felt limp in his.

He began to weep. For her. For himself. For his failure as a psychiatrist. For falling so desperately in love with Eleanor when his wife was so sick. Yet, mustn't he move on? Was not life to be lived? He would have asked God to help him at that moment, but he no longer believed. He looked upon his wife. What kind of God could cause such suffering?

Charles returned from Mountain Grove Hospital for Dipsomania and Inebriates eight weeks later. He was quiet and somber a good deal of the time. Eleanor felt certain he must be reliving his stay at the hospital. No one said a word about the next step for him, fearing approaching the topic and agitating him.

Colin finally got his own apartment, a tiny flat on Temple Street, within walking distance to the mill but still visited often.

"Well, Charles, what do you think is next for you now that you're better and fit as a fiddle?" He spoke lightly.

"I've been thinking about that and believe I'd like to be involved with the mill again, believe it or not. I can be of great help there. I can always study landscape architecture on my own and apply it to my own grounds. Sort of as a hobby."

Colin raised his brows. "Now that's a surprise. I'd of thought you'd take some courses Eleanor mentioned to me."

"Truthfully, I think I'd feel out of place with all those younger people. And I'd rather stay close by. I've got all I need to keep me busy here in my own garden, with Tom's help."

Eleanor came into the room. "And truthfully, gardening would be more in spring and summer. I think it would be wonderful for you to return to work at the mill. With your experience you'll do a fine job there. And the men respect you. Your advice would be invaluable. Flanagan would welcome your help with open arms."

"There's talk of a strike though."

"Nothin' new there."

"I'll mention it to Flanagan tomorrow and you can set up an appointment. He's tryin' to be fairer with the workers and profits from commission weavin'. He set up a payment plan for the weavers to pay off their looms, a fair one, so they can take home a decent salary. Some of the mills went the other way and have turned out, as they call them, to be cockroach shops. It's disgusting how they take advantage of the workers."

Charles rose. "Well, that's settled then. Let's drink to it."

Eleanor and Colin froze.

Charles smiled. "I was thinking of some iced tea or coffee, or lemonade."

Eleanor rushed to the kitchen, floating with joy. Their relationship had improved since he returned, though not sexually. She still felt frightened by the thought of sex but was quite good at not showing it. At least she thought so. And Charles threw himself deeply into his work at the mill.

It seemed "the cure" had worked.

Ironically, she had Kirov to thank for suggesting it.

Charles enjoyed his new job. He was placed in charge of all orders for silk for the mill since he had become an expert. With one glance he could tell the difference between good silk and the flawed variety so many merchants tried to pass off.

Charles knew his experience was invaluable in many ways. He was given other responsibilities as well, assigned to train two men on the characteristics of Japanese raw silk—its small amount of boil off, its white and creamy color, its absence of hard gums, generally well made, cross reeled and convenient in size and weight. Then he taught the men thrown silk sizing, the proportionate values of thrown silk at different boil off, how to read tables for measuring humidity in worsted and cotton yards, for numbering cotton yarn and spun silk. He was also responsible for yarn counts, belting, checking size and speed of pulleys, setting up tables of list prices and weights of steel shafting.

His salary was excellent, commensurate with his responsibilities. Yet, he felt overwhelmed by all this work load. He spoke to no one for fear he would seem weak.

More and more he longed for a drink to calm him down.

Eleanor did not notice this. She had become more and more interested in women's suffrage in the spare hours she could manage. Since the ratification of the 19th Amendment which had finally given women the right to vote, she wished Mary could have lived to see the advances in women's rights. She tried not to think of Mary on the one hand; it was too painful. She still became paralyzed with sadness at her loss. On the other hand, she felt a sense of wrong in not thinking of her and tried to make her life at the Alliance a living memorial to her.

Another strike began with twenty thousand silk workers unsuccessfully battling against a proposed four-loom system. It seemed Eleanor was living the Great Silk Strike of 1913 all over again. But this one was the final blow to the silk industry as the manufacturers interpreted it. They were in complete disgust with the constant labor disputes that plagued Paterson and started to actively look for new sites in other cities where the workers were not as militant and the taxes were lower, as well as power being less expensive. Eleanor was on pins and needles during the strike for fear it would put Charles over the edge with nothing to do; but, thankfully, it was of short duration and certainly did not approach the near starvation, violence and suffering that occurred during the strike of 1913.

Eleanor's love for Kirov grew stronger and stronger but she fought it. They met as often as they could. He asked to become the Women's Alliance doctor once again. Both felt an overwhelming need to be near each other. Dr. Swenson, whose major loyalty lay with St. Joseph's where he had interned and been a doctor for fifteen years, was more than happy to oblige.

But after a time doubt enveloped her. There was no getting around what they were doing was wrong. It bothered her and she knew it did Kirov as well.

They met in Hawthorne that Saturday.

"How can we continue? I can't bear it when you leave the Alliance, knowing I won't see you again until tomorrow." She rubbed her hands against her dress. "And then I must face Charles so kind and good. And I know what you are going through as well."

She gazed out the windows at the wild flowers now all abloom in what looked like an early summer.

"We should be—husband and wife. There. I've said it." She saw the sadness in his eyes as he spoke.

"We know that can never be. Especially now that Charles has improved. How could I live with myself if he relapsed?"

"And Anna. I see her face before me and feel such pain."

"We can't go on this way. This guilt will kill us."

He half smiled. "Why do we have to be so moral?"

"We must separate. We must. Guilt will destroy us in the end. And you seem to be against seeing Dr. Brodky to help you. In fact," he hesitated, I'm thinking of seeing someone myself. I'm torn apart by this relationship. And it is affecting my life and shouldn't be."

"All right then." she sighed.

He walked toward her, his shoulders hunched.

She held him hard, felt his heart pounding against hers. The roots of her heart seemed to connect to his as surely as air to breath. How would they survive if this was the last time they would be together when what they both lived for was to see each other again?

Time passed. The twenties were the time of "runnin' wild." The Charleston became the rage and skirts were shorter, hair was bobbed in the new style. Clara Bow, Nazimova, Pola Negri, Charles Farrell and Janet Gaynor were idols at the box office. The mah jong craze was fun and in full bloom. Charles became interested in jazz and bought all of Louis Armstrong's records as well as Bessie Smith's and Eleanor became enamoured of Edna St. Vincent Millay's sonnets, this new writer, F. Scott Fitzgerald and his book, *This Side of Paradise*, Jean Toomer's *Cane* which she felt proud to discover since it was not that well known and the librarian had suggested it. Charles was more interested in the Clarence Darrow case and the possibility Lindbergh would actually fly across the Atlantic, which he considered completely impossible. She, Charles, and Colin went to see *The Jazz Singer*, the very first talking picture and were so impressed they hardly spoke when they came home.

And Aaron and Eleanor, though they used some of these diversions to stave off their heartache, remained true to their promise of not seeing each other. Eleanor encouraged Charles in every way she could. But she lived death in life without Kirov. She longed for the unannounced times he would appear at the Alliance and knew he did too. Yet, she did feel more calm in her life in another way, not having to live with the guilt and betrayal of two perfectly decent people, both so frail. Perhaps the situation might have been different if their spouses were not so delicate.

Colin, no fool, saw the great change in Eleanor. Once again she hardly ate; her face had a strange, hollow look. Her green eyes seemed glazed at times. But Charles was better now. Her fears for him could not be the reason.

Was there something more to her malaise? This mystery must be solved. And he would find its answer, though he felt great fear concerning where it would lead him.

Summer that year came in full glory. The force that propelled the garden to die and return always inspired Eleanor and she was feeling somewhat better. Her garden never disappointed her. The oak leaf hydrangeas hung in large clusters, the bee balm rose towards heaven, her reliable black-eyed Susans returned in swaths of yellow throughout the garden, tucked amidst her faithful sedum. Even the salvia refused to stop blooming in purple spikes.

She loved to walk through this garden just as much as the one she had on Silk Road, alone now rather than with Charles. He always brought work home, it seemed. Yet, he was working in the greenhouse quite often again and that gave her great hope. He needed the comfort of creating life from the soil as much as she did.

Then, to everyone's surprise, rain came. Not just the usual rain that people tolerated, especially gardeners, but eight days of it that flooded out the Passaic River, which overflowed its banks and was totally merciless in flooding out Paterson, especially the area near the Great Falls where the mills were inundated with water and irreparable damage. Market Street, Main Street, Water Street, River Street, the lower portion of Ryle Avenue and Temple Street got the brunt of damage from the flooding. At first it seemed containable but then in a flash overflowed its banks onto River Street. As it progressed, it flooded the trolley lines and transportation halted. Its torrents lashed through Paterson Street to Straight Street. Companies along its route of devastation brought in rowboats to evacuate its employees, taken off guard by the water's force and danger.

As the days passed, the torrents did not subside and the water reached as far north as North First Street. Water lay three feet high in the streets as many homeowners scrambled to move their furniture, and themselves, to the upper floors of their houses for the duration of the flooding. Men and women wept as the Passaic River lashed through the streets carrying large amounts of debris—strollers, planters, lamps, chairs, gardening utensils, hoses, lawn chairs, so much else—watching as it got bottlenecked and stuck against the Broadway and Main Street Bridge girders.

On the eastern side of the river, the water reached Governor Street. It was common now to see rowboats carrying people across the river, older children seeming the only people unconcerned about the tragedy as they splashed each other in the water, oblivious to the backed-up sewers that were enlarging the area of flooding to Washington and Godwin Street. People began to live in fear the Arch Street bridge would collapse.

Still the rain would not stop and the flood water continued, reaching further, almost to Fair and Bridge Streets. The engine company on Water Street had to evacuate and moved to a dry spot on Temple Street hill.

The greatest concern for Charles and Colin was the clogged mill raceway intake gates at the Passaic River near Spruce Street. If the floodwater reached the raceway system, the flooding would thoroughly destroy the heart of the mill district below, not to mention the locomotive shops.

Plans were made to dynamite Spruce Street, sealing the adjacent raceway. Mercifully, this was not necessary, but not before the mills suffered great damage, losing their entire stock.

After the eighth day, the rains subsided. Charles and Colin left for the mill area via rowboat to survey the devastation to Flanagan's Silk Mill. Inside, the machines sat in a few feet of water, silk lay in giant skeins, ruined. Charles knew that among the myriad causes that combine to keep down the production of a silk mill below what should be expected, one of the most important is an unfavorable atmospheric environment. No fiber is more affected by moisture than silk and moisture present in silk under normal conditions will vary—its locality, season of the year, even from day to day.

The Japanese raw silk, so precious for weaving, lay wet and soaked beyond use. Charles picked up a skein, grew misty-eyed.

"No shame in a man showing his sadness," Colin said quietly. "But we'll rebuild. You'll see. Be back to work before you know it."

Colin was no fool. He knew Charles' fear that with nothing to do but think he could relapse.

Charles frowned. "No, we won't. This is the end of Paterson and its silk mills. What with the strikes, cheaper labor elsewhere, what owner in his right mind will invest all the money needed to start all over again?" He sighed. "We are witnessing the beginning of the end of the silk industry in Paterson."

They returned to the rowboat, sullen faced, as were all the other workers and owners in rowboats who had come and gone from various mills to witness what appeared to be the beginning of their end.

Charles dropped Colin off at his apartment.

"I've got a few chores to do. I won't be long. Tell Eleanor, will you, when you stop by? I want to see how the other mills fared."

He rowed slowly towards a building where he knew the password and could get in, bought a bottle of whiskey and tucked it neatly into the inner pocket of his raincoat.

One drink. That would be it.

Colin caught a bad cold, most likely from the dampness and germs at the mill. It worsened into what appeared to be the flu. Eleanor administered various medicines from the Alliance and made sure he drank plenty of liquids. Yet, he began to feel so sick he hardly drank or ate.

"I hate this troublin' you," he complained. "But I think you were right. I need a doctor. I feel like I'm on fire."

"I'll call Dr. Swenson at St. Joseph's."

"No, I want Dr. Kirov. I like the man. He knows what he's doing." Eleanor stood immovable. "But—I don't think he makes house calls anymore. For months now. He's too busy at St. Joseph's and the Alliance."

"I think he'd stop by for me."

"I don't think—" She suddenly realized the tray she held with his soup was shaking in her hands.

Charles took it from her. "I just hope you're not coming down with something as well."

"I'm tired. That's all."

"I'll call Dr. Kirov for you then."

"But—"

Before she could stop him, Charles left the room, contacted Kirov, who said he would stop by immediately after his visits with his patients.

"Did you tell him who you were?"

Charles frowned. "That's a strange question. Of course I did. I do think you're coming down with something."

"Will you handle things when he arrives? I'm tired and do want to lie down. But I'm not sick."

"Of course, my dear, of course I will."

Colin was shocked when he saw Kirov. He had lost more weight and his jacket had stains on it. The cuffs of his shirt were soiled. But his presence was still commanding as it had been when Colin first encountered him.

He met with Charles after seeing Colin.

"I'm glad you called. Your father-in-law has pneumonia. I gave him an injection and a bottle of medicine which you must begin giving him immediately. Hopefully, we won't have to hospitalize him."

Charles wondered why Kirov kept looking towards the front door.

"Before you leave, could you examine my wife? I'm probably over reacting but I love her dearly and she's so stubborn. Doesn't want to see you. You remember her. She works at the Alliance. When I was away, you took care of her. May have saved her life."

"If she doesn't show serious symptoms and doesn't want me to see her—"

"Insists she's fine. Of course, between us, she hasn't been herself for monthss. She's subject to severe depression. But now she's becoming more frail physically as well."

Kirov looked as though he had received a blow to the face.

"Are you all right?"

"My—stomach's been acting up, I'm afraid."

"It would just take a moment for me to get you some tea."

"No, thank you. I'll be fine. I must admit if she insists she doesn't want to see a doctor perhaps by day after tomorrow when I return you can convince her if her symptoms worsen. I don't like to interfere unless the patient is cooperative. You understand. Unless, of course, I must."

"All right then. Until the day after tomorrow."

Kirov thought long and hard on the way home. He knew Eleanor feared seeing him outside the Alliance, never alone. But worse still, he feared it too.

Kirov kept his promise to visit Colin in a few days and he was vastly improved. Eleanor managed to stay in the kitchen most of the time baking. Colin thought that strange, that she not even greet him, since they were colleagues at the Alliance. He supposed she wanted Charles to feel in charge. Anything either of them could do these days to make him feel needed was certainly tried. With the mill closed indefinitely, he sat around the house moping, Colin and Eleanor on pins and needles he might start drinking again. He slept a great deal and worked in the greenhouse more, but that did not make them suspicious. Of course, he would be terribly depressed at the devastation of Flanagan's and seemed to be coping well enough.

"Well, it looks like Colin's fine, according to Dr. Kirov. A few more days and he'll be his old self again." Charles embraced Eleanor while she continued cooking.

"I don't doubt Colin will be looking for work at another mill. I understand Dougherty's and Weinberg's aren't as bad off being somewhat farther from the river. A man who came to the Alliance with a fever told me that yesterday. I'll tell him. He may want to switch mills. Who knows?"

"I won't work anywhere but Flanagan's. Those mills all have their own ways and managers. No need of me. And I know everyone there. I sometimes think he hired me because of Kosinski's recommendation. Plus, of course he knew my father."

"I doubt that. You're a talented man. I wish you'd believe in yourself more than you do. Why, look at all you accomplished when you took over the mill after your father died. All your caring for the workers. Thousands turning out at the baby's funeral."

She gasped. It was an unspoken agreement they not speak of their child.

He turned to leave.

"I have to go out a while, just for a breath of air and some cigars."

Eleanor smiled. "It'll do you some good."

If she had known his destination, her smile would have turned to tears.

She served dinner as usual that evening.

Colin smiled. "Kirov gave me a clean bill of health. Finally. I need to find work. I'll be glad of it, back at my own apartment. I hated havin' to put you two out with all you have on your minds."

"I'm glad you're better."

"Shame about Dr. Kirov, isn't it?"

"A shame?"

"He's leavin' St. Joseph's. Personal reasons he told me. So you'll need another doctor at the Alliance."

She plopped onto the kitchen chair.

"Now, don't you worry. They'll get another doctor to take his place."

Take his place? No one could ever take his place. She sat at the dinner table watching Colin and Charles drink their tea.

And then she made her decision.

She knew where Kirov lived from his file at St. Joseph's, easy enough to look up during her visits to and from the hospital regarding patients, 114 Lane Street, a few blocks above the river, an area which, though a few steps above the tenement area where she lived in her younger years, was not much better.

She walked slowly up the stairs to his apartment, aware-ness and certainty in each step. Her soft knock on the door sounded like a gong to her. She stood breathless, her heart pumping faster and faster.

"Who is it?" His voice, so comforting. It had been so long they dared speak to each other except concerning patients.

She did not answer. She knocked again.

"Who is it?" Still she could not speak her name, felt mute.

Finally, he opened the door. The frown upon his face turned to a look of shock.

"May I come in?"

"Such a question. Of course."

They held each other a time. In his arms she felt she could touch the heavens.

"Colin said you're leaving St. Joseph's. The Alliance. You can't leave. You can't!"

"I must. I can't go on this way." He stared at his body. "Look at me. The weight I've lost. I can hardly eat. It takes all my strength to get through the day. And you? You're so thin and look exhausted." He gently touched the area beneath her eyes. "Dark circles. No. It's better I leave and start a new life.

I'm torn by my predicament every day. It's destroying both of us. I must move on, start out elsewhere. God knows where or how I can."

"And what about me? I can't let you go. I can't. We must be together again. We were foolish to separate. We haven't hurt anyone. We'll be totally discreet. Aaron, I can not live without you."

He led her to the bedroom. Their clothes were almost removed by the time they got there. As usual, she was terrified at first but did not show it. But their love-making, the culmination of so many months of denial, overwhelmed both of them. The passion she felt for Kirov lay requited for such a time it soared through her. All her reasons for not being with him were brushed away. She would not deny herself again.

She stayed with him many hours. Her mind was made up.

Kirov would be in her life.

"Have you thought about working with the the psychiatrist I mentioned to you a while back? I see you at the Alliance and I can hardly bear to see the depression that emanates from you at times, though you have become an expert at disguising it."

"I have decided. I can't bear this suffering, this confusion any longer. I will work with him if you think I should. There are so many demons I must conquer to be free of guilt. And shame. My childhood. I never told you so many other things about it. I know now I need someone, a trained person—I think of Ann Dodge's miraculous recovery. Yes, I need help. I admit it. I've been reading Freud and his belief in childhood trauma and how it can affect a person. I want to be rid of these demons when I come to you, at least to understand them. You deserve no less."

He held her hard. "And so it's settled then, my darling. I will make the proper arrangements."

Charles walked at a fast pace towards the area he knew so well where the speakeasy was located. Sweat lay on his brow. His hands trembled.

He waited for Kosinski as he turned into the alleyway. He was back to drinking as well. The closing of the mill, the responsibility of supporting a wife who now took in ironing, the children to support, had taken its toll and gave him a perfect excuse to drink himself to oblivion. It did not occur to him that the money he spent on liquor could have been used to support his family. And when it did, it was easy to rationalize his deserving to have those drinks to help him get through the day. His rationalization served a major purpose in Charles' downhill slide. Each fed upon the other's excuses.

The speakeasy was bustling with activity. Flappers shimmied around the room, liquor poured in abundance.

"Police!" The sound of a club on the door was deafening.

"Open the door by order of the Volstead Act!" The dreaded act gave police the power to enforce Prohibition. And they did just that, breaking down the door.

The pounding at the door made everyone freeze at first, then scurry towards the windows which were nearly too high to get through, though one or two made it, as Charles and Kosinski stood hopelessly in line to exit through the window. Before they realized it, they were being led, then pushed into the police van but not before Charles was able to drink as long as possible from the bottle on the bar.

It would have to last him a long time.

Eleanor arrived home in the early hours of the morning. She had no idea what she would tell Charles and was, for a few moments, grateful he was not home but soon suspicious there could be only one reason he wasn't. Yet, he might have been delayed for a number of valid reasons. Somehow she did not want to interrupt the memory of the glorious moments she knew in the arms of Kirov with her trials with Charles.

She woke up early that morning with a call from the police he was in jail and to come down to the station. Colin insisted on going with her, but she would not allow it. She would be all right, though her heart was heavy from Charles' setback.

The happiness she'd know with Kirov had already been swept away.

Charles looked out of place, one of the few men in a tailored suit, sitting amidst so many flannel-shirted, heavy-set workmen whose red-veined faces belied many years of drinking.

He approached the cell door, shamefaced.

"Eleanor."

"I have nothing to say to you right now. I've bailed you out. We'll talk later. We're both exhausted." She noticed his hands trembling. Why hadn't she observed that happening again? Because of Kirov. He occupied her mind and soul constantly. But she refused to blame herself and fall into one of the dark depressions constantly waiting to strike her.

When they arrived home, Colin was there and sitting at the kitchen table.

"You've got to get back to the hospital All it was was a slip. It can happen to any man."

"It's the mill. Your boredom." Eleanor tried to be understanding, partially from her own guilt regarding Kirov. And she knew from workers from the mill who came to the Alliance the tremendous grip alcohol can have on a person.

"I'll never go back to the hospital. Never. I can stop on my own. I'm certain of it."

"I don't think that's possible. You have to get help, go back."

"I'll just have to prove it to you then, won't I?"

She felt too exhausted and confused from the last twenty-four hours to disagree.

"I'm going to bed."

She climbed the stairs slowly, wishing Kirov was holding her in the comfort of his arms, telling her what to do. And then depression overwhelmed her. She took two sleeping pills and fell into a sound sleep. Charles continued to be in complete denial over his addictive drinking and had taken to reading the Bible lately upon his return, as was suggested at the rehabilitation center. Eleanor felt at her wit's end and that it was useless to send him back to Mountain Grove against his adamant pleading he could stop on his own. And so they continued to play a cat and mouse game with her constantly pretending she was not watching his every move and his pretending he was in complete control of his drinking.

She awakened the next morning to find Colin standing above her. "I'm off to the asylum today. Do you want to come?"

"Of course."

She hated the thought of the possibility of seeing Anna Kirov again, the guilt she would experience, but that must not deter her from the humane act of visiting her aunt.

The asylum looked more foreboding this time, a great deal of that from the dank November day. A gray sky hovered above them and refused to show even a patch of sun. The misty, damp day was not conducive to the atmosphere the asylum attempted to project to begin with; its fortress-like appearance seemed to verify its function.

The matron led them to Colleen's quarters. The visit was in its way calming, for she sat in her own world of delusion and Colin sat, as she did, talking to her, finally succumbing to silence. Once in a while Colleen smiled at the wall.

A while later the matron entered with the guard.

"Time for some exercise. You can go with her if you like."

As the matron tried to get the inmates first to lift their left arm, then right and so on, most of them stood immobile or sat on the floor. But she seemed to feel this was what she was paid to do, and she tried her best.

Eleanor soon spotted Anna Kirov sitting on the floor. After the exercise time was over, against Colin's wishes, she felt compelled to approach her.

"Anna, you don't know me. But I know someone who loves you very much. Your husband, Aaron." Tears filled her eyes. Anna did not notice. "He's such a good man. A good doctor. He wants you to get well. Do you understand?" The woman's gaze met Eleanor's and Eleanor clasped her hand. "If only you could speak, if only you could understand, he could be free of his guilt. And so could I." She tightened her grasp on Anna's hand. Anna scratched deeply into her wrist, drawing blood.

Eleanor pulled away in shock.

Had she understood what she said? Or had she become angry at her holding her hand?

Anna laughed, then screamed so loud she drew the attention of those around her. Colin ran over as he saw Eleanor's fingers bathed in blood as she held her arm.

"What the—" He stared at the woman laughing hysterically. And then he saw her name tag pinned to her dress. "Oh, God." He crouched down next to Eleanor. "Is she Kirov's—?"

"His wife."

He helped Eleanor rise as the guard approached.

Gus Mott had worked at the asylum two years, the longest he ever held a job. He was a man who spent his life with a grudge in his heart. He'd had an abusive father who often came home drunk and beat him, often for the most trivial reasons, while his mother stood trembling, fearful of interfering. It also did not help that he was a short, pudgy mean, his main pride a tattoo, an anchor on his left forearm. He felt his masculinity soar each time he and others studied it and complimented him on it.

He threw his cigarette to the ground and crushed it. This job at the asylum was a dream come true for him. His wife, who was going through menopause, had refused him any sexual relationship as long as he could remember, unless he forced himself upon her. He was a man who had great sexual needs and the asylum was a perfect place for fulfilling them. After all, what harm did it do to the "loonies," as he referred to them. They were completely oblivious to his advances so what harm did it do?

Of course he had his favorite, the Kirov "loony." What a beauty she was and as crazy as they come. He sometimes thought she had a look of terror in her eyes when he entered her, but he knew that had to be impossible. Yet, she tried to avoid him.

He refused to stop thinking about it. Action was his goal in life, not thought and feeling and he rushed to Eleanor's side.

"I'm so sorry, ma'am. My eyes got to be in the back of my head in this place. Do you want to see our nurse to get looked at?"

"No. I'll be all right," she managed, though shaken to the core.

Anna lunged at the guard.

He was the man who had thrown her to the ground, lifted her dress, took off her panties and ripped her vagina open as he lay on top of her when he raped her.

But she would win in the end.

She had stolen something from his pocket during his ecstasy which would finally free her.

Colin tried to calm Eleanor down as they approached the trolley that would take them to Paterson. When they arrived home, she avoided Charles and asked that her dinner be brought to her room.

It did not take much insight for Colin to understand why she was so troubled to see Anna Kirov and why she refused to see Kirov the day he visited when he was so sick. And his desire to leave St. Joseph's, which would also include the Alliance.

Charles was in his study, just beginning to doze off, which made Colin suspicious. Dinner hadn't even been served yet. But he held his tongue.

"We had quite an experience at the asylum today."

Charles rubbed his eyes and sat up straight.

"What happened?"

"We saw Kirov's wife."

"Poor woman. She was visiting a relative there as well?"

"No. It's his wife that's there. Mad as a hatter. She attacked Eleanor when she tried to comfort her."

Charles perked up. "Is she all right? Where is she?"

"Upstairs. Wants to dine in her room so I think she must be somewhat shaken."

"Well," Colin began cautiously. "I finally put the puzzle together why you went back to drink. You could have confided in me, you know. It wasn't mostly the mill, was it? It's Eleanor and Kirov. Their affair."

Charles did not speak or move.

"And if you don't get yourself together again like you promised, I can't say what will happen. It all fits now. How she's tried to avoid him, God knows. The night he came. And the weight loss and depression. Her confusion over you or Kirov. Right before my own eyes and I didn't see it. Why didn't you share your burden with me? And what do you plan to do about it?"

Charles still could not speak, then cleared his throat. "I—" He could say no more.

"Fight, Charles. That's what you have to do. You can win her back. God knows she loves you or she wouldn't be in the confusion she's in, now would she? After what you two have been through together."

Colin thought surely Charles would speak. But still he did not. Had he been drinking?

Colin squeezed his shoulder. "You can beat this. You need to go to the hospital again. Eleanor would be glad of it and it would show you're serious about gettin' better. If you can straighten yourself out, I'm convinced she's yours. I believe that. One thing I do know. She'll never desert you. Never."

Charles placed his elbows on his knees, clenched his fingers around his forehead. "I—I don't know—what to say."

"You don't have to say anything now. Just think about it."

"I will. Long and hard."

"It's all I ask. Eleanor means the world to me. I want her happiness above all things. And if you straighten yourself out, you can give it to her."

"I'll try. Harder than I've ever tried to do anything in my life."

After Colin left, Charles went to the library, removed a few books from one shelf, found the bottle of whiskey and drank much of it.

He went to the window and stared at the garden a long time. It was in decline. Autumn leaves, usually so colorful, had dried out, and piles of them covered the lawn. The hydranga hung limp, its leaves and flowers dry as paper. The black-eyed Susans, sedum, bee balm, roses, iris, so many others were brittle. He felt the sterility of the garden overpowering him and a rush of sadness so deep he moaned.

Eleanor and Kirov. How could he not have known?

"Let's go, Anna," the aide said. "Don't give me that blank stare. I dealt with enough crazies to know from studyin' you you're crazy but not as crazy as they think. Most don't fight goin' in the baths. Don't even know or remember bein' in them. Not like you. You do, don't yuh?"

Anna pushed hard against the aide's chest to no avail, and he began to lead her towards the giant hydrotherapy room where a female aide waited, with its icy tubs of water, above each a suspended hammock where she would be placed after being tightly wrapped. According to Dr. Gold's instructions she was to be immersed for two hours, bandages wrapped tightly around her body, like a frozen mummy.

The aide turned the dials and gauges according to Dr. Gold's instructions, forty degrees in her case, and he manipulated the flow of water on her, just as the doctor ordered. Every day she was placed in the tub, tied to the hammock, suspended, the canvas sheet covering every part of her, except her head, lowered into the icy water. Then she would be placed in the "needle box" where they sat her as high pressure water stung her skin directly.

She heard Dr. Gold saying to a colleague, also a great believer as most of the psychiatrists were, in cerebral congestion and hydrotherapy; this was a supposedly proven way to act upon the vascular system, eliminating its impurities, whatever that meant.

She stared at her smock on its hook on the wall. How could she have left her stolen treasure in its pocket? She should have hidden it under her mattress.

The aide began to bind her. Then she placed her in the hammock, plunged her into the icy water. Numbness permeated her. But it was far better than having her tonsils, ovaries, fallopian tubes removed as they had done with her room mate. Those procedures hadn't brought improvement either. The next step would be that process for her, she knew, if this one did not help. The removal of her teeth did nothing.

Yet, she felt hope. Soon she would be free of this suffering. If her plan worked.

No, she was not quite as crazy as they thought.

The New Year began. Eleanor was glad, hoped it would be a time for new beginnings. But as the months passed as she was going over the ledger of the Alliance she could plainly see the loss column was much higher than the profit one. She must ask Charles for more money. She had no desire to profit from the Alliance, just to break even. It seemed immoral to make a profit from others' misery. But she did have to keep the books balanced. The salary to Nora and Brigitte, plus cost for supplies, medications, sheets, soaps, so much else, continued to outweigh heavily the meager amounts the mill workers gave her as payments. Some had past due accounts in arrears over a year. How could she ask or for that matter take their money when they could hardly put food on their tables? So many of the men, and now more prevalent after the flood, turned to alcohol and came home with even less for their wives to use on food, clothing, rent. She felt nothing but the greatest gratitude and love for Kirov who would not take one penny in salary.

She placed her head on the desk and began to cry. Would she ever be free of memories that haunted her every day? She was certain now Charles was back to drinking and saw no way out of the situation. She felt it approaching, the heavy, dull thud in her head she lived with for years, a precursor to depression. She would fight to her heart's core not to become immobile in bed again, to hide her suffering. She must try to stand up, a monumental task, ready herself to leave. Yet, that heaviness struck, causing her difficulty in rising from her desk, kept trying to overpower her.

She decided to rest her head just a few more minutes upon the desk. Yet now she sensed hope. If this Doctor Brodsky was half as understanding as Kirov, perhaps he could help her. She knew nothing about psychoanalysis, except what she had read in books and was many times ddidfficult to comprehend. But she must trust Kirov. Yet, there was so much to conquer, her childhood sexual abuse, her memories of the beatings, her guilt over the death of her mother, the death of her child, her leaving Charles for Dante Ravelli, her relatioship with Charles and Aaron. Should she choose him or Kirov? Could she trust this psychiatrist? What would he be like? Soon the few minutes became an hour or so when she fell sound asleep to oblivion. Blessed sleep to take her away from her misery.

Anna watched her room mate, Charlotte, carefully as the orderlies took her with them for the lobotomy. She knew all about it, for she listened astutely to every word, every sound that clanged in her ears constantly. Sometimes above the clanging she learned a great deal from the aides, nurses, doctors.

She heard them now as they conferred about a procedure on a patient. They said the older method of lobotomizing would not be used. She heard of patients who had their skull drilled into and an instrument placed in, much like an apple corer. The doctors complained sometimes for often they could not see where or what they were cutting. The fibers of the frontal lobes, when severed, caused irreparable damage. But Dr. Zimmer read of a newer, more efficient procedure of shocking the patient with electrodes to her temples, the left eyelid lifted, and an ice pick placed through the eye. This led to their experimentation with lobotomies at the asylum, as the patients who had any awareness waited in terror to see who would be next.

Charlotte was to be operated on by Dr. Gold. They had tried every procedure with her, including sleep therapy, injecting her with the barbiturate Somnifene. She had slept four weeks, being awakened only for food. But prolonged narcosis, as they called the procedure, had failed. Anna heard Dr. Gold telling a nurse he was grateful it had not induced a fatal coma, which it had been known to do.

Lobotomy was the last resort.

Two female orderlies led Charlotte down the hall where they were met by a nurse.

"Now, Charlotte, you won't know a thing when it's over. It'll be for the best. Just you wait and see."

All was still this early morning. Quietude and emptiness filled the air. The patients were still asleep, most drugged from their medications and treatments.

But Anna fooled the nurse. Last night she put her pill under her tongue and spit it out as soon as the nurse left. Ironically, she had the best sleep she had in months. She dreamed she was back home again, that she was holding her darling newborn daughter and her parents were there, alive and healthy, smiling, as Aaron stood admiringly above her. She opened the top of her lace and silk dress and removed her breast to let her daughter drink from it. Mother and child, father and family, all filled with joy.

But then another dream followed. A monster followed her. She was in a cave and tried to run out but could hardly walk. She turned, saw one of a giant demon's heads had squeezed through the hole of the cave. She tried to run but her legs would only allow her to walk. Sweat broke out on her forehead. She turned again. The monster had wedged its second head through the entrance. She stumbled, her body soaked with sweat. She turned, saw a third head emerging through the cave's entrance as the demon stood full length in front of her, his mouth dripping saliva through fanged teeth.

She screamed, then awakened.

The night nurse arrived, calmed her down. "It's only a dream, Anna. Try to get back to sleep."

After the night nurse left, she lay on her bed thinking what her future would be here. Then the voices took over. Laughing. Always laughing at her.

She thought of Charlotte being taken away to the North Wing, of her fate.

That would not be hers. She put on her smock. She felt the matches she had stolen from the guard in her pocket. She took them out and lighted one. Her smock quickly caught fire. She felt the excruciating pain from the flames rushing into her skin, to her arms, chest, neck, face.

She slumped on the floor, immolated.

She died with a smile upon her face.

"Eleanor! Wake up!"

Colin stood above her and, bleary eyed, she began to rub her eyes, awaken.

"Did I fall asleep so long?"

"I got a call from Kirov. It's quite terrible. Horrible."

She jumped up from the chair.

"Is he all right?"

"I don't know. I doubt it."

She sank back onto the chair.

"His wife. She burned to death in a fire at the asylum. They think she started it. Destroyed half the Third Ward before they got it under control. Over twenty's dead. He called to tell me Colleen is dead. Her cell. They found two bodies. Most are burned to the point you can't identify them. Except for the cell they were trapped in."

She could see his hands shake as he spoke.

"Good God, how did she ever get matches?"

"Nobody knows. She must of stole them somehow from a guard or nurse or doctor. That we'll never know."

Eleanor clenched her forehead.

"Kirov. He must be devastated. And Aunt Colleen…"

She went to the cabinet poured a glass of wine, drank it, offered one to Colin who drank it immediately.

"What did he say? I suppose he called you because of Colleen."

"No. He asked for you. But you weren't home."

Eleanor did not speak.

Colin sighed. "I know, Eleanor. I've known for a time. Didn't take much to put two and two together when I thought about it."

"Know?"

"You and Kirov. That you're very much in love. Now with this I don't know what'll happen. How he'll handle the death of his wife in such a terrible way. You have to be ready for that."

"His guilt. We've lived with it. Both of us, for so long. But this. We never dreamed of this. What did he say?"

"That he had to take care of things regarding Anna. And not to contact him."

"Not to contact him?"

"Eleanor, there's Charles to think of. He needs you. Kirov told me to tell you—he's going away and had no idea when he would be back. He's a moral person. You know that. He's got to work out his guilt, I think, on the one hand, and his love for you on the other."

"Going away?" She grasped her hands. "But where?"

"He wouldn't say."

She jumped from the chair. "I've got to see him before he goes. I have to."

He grabbed her arm. "It's no use. He has to work this out— alone." He handed her an envelope. "He told me to give you this." At last he would explain his reasons for leaving, tell her where he had gone. She opened it and it was a scrap of paper that said: "Nathan Brodsky, Psychiatrist, 118 26th Avenue, Paterson, New Jersey." She turned the paper over.

It was blank.

She broke free from Colin, ran across town to Kirov's apartment. It was dark when she arrived, and she was only guided by the glow of the street lamps. She ran up the stairs to his flat, pounded on the door.

"Aaron!"

She pounded it until her palms were red and stinging, calling his name.

No one answered.

PART III

She lay in the darkness of her bedroom, feeling eventually he would return. He would not leave her so lost, depressed. At least they could have spoken before he left. But he must not have trusted himself to leave. How she longed to comfort him concerning Anna's death. She deserved to know at least where he was going. Her head felt squeezed by an elastic band becoming tighter and tighter.

She knew now she must see this Dr. Brodsky. She could go on no longer, the years of depression and suffering. And she trusted Kirov completely.

Charles entered holding something in his arms.

"May I open the curtains, brighten the room? I bought you a present. I know how you're feeling with the tragic death of your aunt."

"Of course."

He opened the curtains and crossed the room. He carried a puppy, long eared, curly from head to paws, with liquid brown eyes, beginning to yelp in his arms.

She sat up. He handed the puppy to her. Ever since their last dog had died, she'd mentioned getting another one to Charles.

She immediately fell in love.

"She's adorable. Where ever did you get her?"

"The pet shop on Main. She was sitting in a cage in the window all by herself. I had to have her. For you."

Eleanor held the puppy to her heart and she immediately stopped yelping.

"I see you're her favorite already." He pretended a frown.

"I love her!"

"She'll need constant tending in the beginning. Mary is really our cook and housekeeper, but I'll pay her a bit more to help with training and feeding."

"Nonsense. Why, she's my gift. And I can train and feed her. At least I'll try my best. I'll get a book from the library."

She tossed her legs off the bed, donned her slippers, all the while trying to hold the puppy. "Oh, she's so precious." Tears filled her eyes, "You're so good to me."

"You can never imagine how much I love you. I would do anything—anything—for your happiness."

She touched his cheek. "What shall we name her?"

"What about Lily? For our favorite flower."

"Lily it is. Shall I go down and get your soup and tea and bring it up? Won't you eat, just a little?"

"It's been a time you've been after me to eat, isn't it?"

He blushed. "I don't mind."

"I think I'll try to go down for dinner tonight."

The prospect of getting help seemed to be alleviating her mind.

Charles held her then, with Lily licking his face as well.

But that was all right. Quite all right.

Eleanor did not expect to find the office of Nathan Brodsky in such disarray when she entered it. It was filled with so many journals, books, papers. When he entered he at first seemed to be taller than he was, a short, elfin-faced man, not at all like the one she envisioned who would have a beard and look exactly like Freud. He smiled at her. She responded to his elfin-faced look immediately.

After she gave him an overview of her problems, he suggested they work three times a week. She gushed forth everything—her sexual abuse by her so called father, her killing her alleged father because of it, her leaving her child for Dante Ravelli and her guilt over it, the death of her child for which she felt terrible guilt, the death of her mother, Charles' drinking, so much of the misery in her life she could not let go.

Dr. Brodsky listened carefully, attempting to alleviate her guilt over circumstances that were not of her making.

"Each of these topics must be dealt with separately.

You have had a stolen childhood. This situation can stay with us the rest of our lives, that is, unless we do not let it. Let us begin next time by talking about your childhood."

"Why would my alleged father do such a thing?"

"We will discuss that and I will try to answer all your questions and, more importantly, have you answer them. But first you must make me a promise, a promise that you will come to see me three times a week to discuss all of these things you have told me and I will help you to understand them, and get well."

"Yes, doctor, I do promise."

"You must understand I will make no judgment upon you for what you tell me. A psychiatrist is much like a priest that way, I suppose. Anything—anything—you tell me here will never be revealed outside this room."

After searching the piles of paper on his desk, he found his appointment book.

"I shall see you at, say four o'clock Saturday then?"

"Yes. You will. I must improve. I must. I feel now my very life depends on it, though I have told no one the depth of despair I am feeling." Surely if this therapy worked on someone as hopeless as Ann Dodge perhaps it would help her also.

They met at the appointed time.

"Let's begin with your childhood. Tell me about your father."

"He wasn't my real father. Later I found out I was another man's daughter, a man I adore."

"Tell me about the man you lived with during your childhood."

"I hated him. He was a brute. Every Friday night he would go across the street to a bar and come home drunk. My mother and I were terrified of his return."

"And why was that?"

"He beat us. My mother walked with a limp because of it and he—"

Her throat parched.

"Yes. Go on."

"When my mother went to sleep he would come to my room. He abused me since I was five years old."

"No wonder your life has been filled with such depression. We live with acts like that every day of our lives. But we must learn to overcome them and carry on, try to lead productive lives. It's very hard indeed. Is he still alive? Is your mother still living."

"They're both dead. My mother was a saintly person but him—I killed him in the end."

Brodsky showed no sign of reaction.

"I loosened the nails on the banister of the back porch and one night when he was in a stupor and out to grab and beat me I was able to push him through it. He hit the ground and died immediately. I can still see him lying there. And I have no regrets. Should I?"

"Let me say if I were in the same situation I would not hesitate to do the same thing." He rubbed his chin. "And your mother?"

"She died because of me."

"You're being very harsh saying that, don't you think?"

"But it's true. The man who killed her wanted revenge on me. When he tried to attack me at the mill where I worked, I fought back. He lives with a deep scar on his face I'm responsible for. And he chose his revenge against the one person dearest to me. My mother. And the guilt still haunts me."

"Did your mother know of your being sexually abused?"

"I'm quite sure she did. But she looked the other way."

"And so she was not as perfect a mother as your memory of her that causes you such guilt."

"I never thought of it that way."

"We—none of us—are perfect. Just an observation."

"Yet, if it hadn't been for my mother I would never have learned to read, to learn about other worlds besides the mill where I worked."

"You see, as I said—none of us are perfect. We possess a great deal of good in us as well. And you—you need to work on forgiving yourself for something tragic that happened to you that is not your fault. I want you to think about forgiveness between now and our next session. I want you to think about the events in your life you have felt such guilt about when, perhaps, what you should have felt was regret. There is a great different between the two, you know."

Time seemed to have flown as their session ended.

"Will you promise me you will think about what we have spoken about today and try to apply it to the events you have told me of?"

"Yes, I promise." She frowned. "But it will be hard."

"Of course it will. Getting better takes a long, long path."

She sighed.

"We have so much to work on, but I'm determined to feel better."

"That attitude is the one that leads to cure."

The next session came as quickly it seemed to Eleanor as the previous one had passed.

There was silence a time.

"I see you are wearing a wedding band," he began.

"Yes."

She twisted it around her finger.

"And would you say your marriage is a good one?"

"I don't know how to answer that. I mean, sometimes it's good and sometimes it isn't, but since we're being completely truthful, I would say it isn't."

"And why is that?"

"Truthfully, I think it all goes back to the death of our child."

"I am so sorry"

"He had diphtheria but an experienced nurse who lived with us at the time said he was improving, getting better."

Her face reddened. "And so I ran off to be with the man I truly loved at that time, Dante Ravelli. But it didn't work out and I came home to find my child died. My husband, Charles, of course, was shattered. I still think he hasn't forgiven me for leaving to be with another man, Dante Ravelli. Or himself. He brought Robbie to the mill where he surely contracted diptheria."

"And have you forgiven him? Surely he did not realize this when he took the child to the mill.

"No. And I never will. He disobeyed me."

"Forgiveness is healing. You must learn to forgive. You need to tell him that."

"I never will."

"No doubt his guilt manifests itself in destructive ways I would guess."

She arched her brows.

"How did you know that? Yes, it's true. He's become an inebriate and was away a time to get help. He is trying hard to be better. He is a kind and good man to me."

"Ah, but that is different from love. And if the marriage is still not working as well as it should, perhaps he should go back again for rehabilitation. If he truly loves you, I think there is a good chance he would."

"But you see," she hesitated, "I am in love with another man. The guilt from this love is strangling me, knowing Charles is so kind and good."

Brodsky was certain she was referring to Kirov. He knew he was on dangerous ground and must remain objective with her, not reveal he was Kirov's dear friend.

"His wife recently died tragically, and he is also living in a world of guilt, I believe."

"So sad"

"I love him more than life itself."

"Do you see? You have answered your own question about your dilemma."

"But I still don't know what to do. I feel a great obligation to my husband, and now especially he needs me."

"Is that your major criteria for staying with him?"

"Yes, I think it is."

"And this other man. Does he need you as much?"

"Well, he is more independent and strong, more so than my husband. But, yes, I do believe he, too, needs me as much. And I love him dearly."

"You have taken a first step. Admitted your love for one man over another."

He glanced at his watch.

"Time is up, I'm afraid. For our next meeting I want you to list specific actions of each man toward you. Will you do that? And will you think of not which man needs you but which man you need more?"

"That will be so difficult. But yes, of course I will try."

Time passed quickly and each time more and more she regretted leaving his office for he seemed to understand her problems so completely, offering possible, workable solutions to them, advising her that here and now are all we must focus on, practically drilling that into her psyche. She began to gain weight. She looked forward to seeing him for he never condemned her, always listened objectively and advised wisely. It was as though all her life she had lived under the suffocating bell jar of guilt and slowly, very slowly was emerging.

Each time she closed the door, Brodsky sighed. He was determined to help her not only because he suspected his dear friend, Kirov, was in love with her. But, above all, it was his moral duty.

The twenties were years of much prosperity. The decade had opened with the nation's first radio broadcast when it announced the results of the 1920 presidential election between James Cox and Warren Harding. Before long radio was in competition with newspapers and magazines in bringing news to the American people who were fascinated they could actually hear the voices of important people inside their living rooms.

The growth of the auto industry also had a great effect upon Americans. Henry Ford and his mass production methods enabled most Americans to actually own a car. People traveled more and were able to explore places whose photos they had only seen in magazines. Prosperity emerged for this development called for improved roads, more restaurants and good hotels.

Recreation soared. Besides movies starring favorites of Eleanor of Greta Garbo, Theda Bara, Joan Crawford, Mary Pickford and Clara Bow, the twenties were filled with sports heroes and labeled, "The Golden Age of Sports." In baseball the great Babe Ruth hit home runs by the dozens, leading the Yankess to World Series championship. He not only inspired them to the championship but also restored greatness to the game. And baseball was not the only outstanding sport. Red Grange popularized football and the famous coach Knute Rockne guided his team to five undefeated seasons and the running backs known as the "Four Horsemen" ran into sporting legend.

Although it was an exciting time it could not match the exhilaration Eleanor felt when she finally received a letter from Kirov which was delivered to her via the Women's Alliance.

Dearest Eleanor,

> Please forgive me for leaving so quickly without saying goodbye. I was so broken by Anna's tragic death I was almost out of my mind. And all I could think of was fleeing and searching for help to sort this tragedy out, and, in truth, face our relationship head on. And so I came to Vienna and am working with Dr. Fritz Neuhauer who was my mentor when I studied here as well as Nathan Brodsky's.

He has been most helpful. I have been seeing him three times a week.

Yes, psychiatrists break down too.

I think of you every day. What a coward I am for running off without even speaking with you. I can only hope you understand. And perhaps my absence will in its way be good for you if you are working with Dr. Brodsky. I pray you are so that you understand your past and its effect upon you, only between you and Brodsky, of course, until some day you may want to share more with me.

I must work out so many problems, my guilt especially because with the death of Anna I still feel a sense of blame and confusion bringing her to America and for her illness, though I am trying to explore the origins of this working with Dr. Neuhauer. I am, of course, exploring our relationship as well.

Please forgive me for not being stronger for you.

Forgive me my turmoil which I must come to grips with.

I am progressing.

Thine,
Aaron

Guilt. Freud, she had read had much to say on this topic and it helped her understand her deep depressions. Brodsky helped her greatly in understanding the difference between guilt and regret. He had become somewhat of a powerful force in helping her understand herself, that she should feel absolutely no guilt at having been abused as a child and must constantly work on that thought. She told him everything, held back nothing and he listened, advising her, making suggestions at times so she was able to see her problems from a different perspective.

She struggled every day to move on with her busyness at the Alliance and went faithfully three times a week to see Dr. Brodsky. Her feeling of a great burden seemed to have been relieved from her when she returned from each visit. She understood now she was not responsible for her mother's death, must work on the shame she felt over her alleged father's sexual abuse, which was not her fault, as well as her beginning to understand her fear of sex and choice of unavailable men protected her from emotion. They discussed every problem openly and each time they met he gave her further insights. She still felt confusion over Charles' refusal to return to Mountain Grove which she was now in the process of discussing with Dr. Brodsky to receive his insights. And what role would Aaron play in her life? She ached for him every day, bathed in memory. But now working with Dr. Brodsky she felt she could talk through all her feelings with him and move toward solutions.

Lily came tearing into the room, yelping for her dinner. She was glad of the distraction. She lifted the puppy in her arms. Her heart stopped pounding as she held Lily next to her heart.

Colin nursed his beer as he sat at McConnolly's Bar, brooding. He could not shake his sadness. He thought of his memories of Michael Collins whom he idealized and believed more and more perhaps he should return to Ireland and take up the banner for its freedom.

What had he accomplished returning? He decided to leave Flanagan's Silk Mill. He knew he could be paid even higher wages by going back to loom fixing. Plus he was informed more and more "cockroach shops" were springing up where the workers put in abnormally long hours with minimum recompense after their weekly payment for the looms they were required to buy. It was one thing for him to make a living but a man with a wife and four or five children barely made enough to eat. The changes at the mills were turning him sour.

Rumor had it two of them, McCarthy's and Bauman's, were planning on setting shop outside of Paterson, outside of New Jersey for that matter, most likely in Pennsylvania where the owners felt there was little worry of anarchists going against them and inciting the workers in the name of justice. Pennsylvania had been instrumental during Paterson's Great Silk Strike of 1913 as well.

But what about Eleanor? Torn between Charles and Kirov. Never again did he think he would have to know the hell she and Charles went through when she left him a few years back. Charles nearly lost his mind, he loved her so.

Charles had nothing to fall back on now with the mill area where he worked hardest hit. Yet, if Charles could straighten out, Colin truly believed Eleanor would not leave him for Kirov. They had been through too much together. And that bond would seal them in the end.

The house was strangely quiet when Colin arrived to visit. The maid let him in. He had stayed at a bar longer than he expected. Eleanor must have been asleep or resting in her room. And then he heard a low, gutteral sound coming from the living room.

He found Charles on the sofa, passed out, an empty bottle of liquor on the table. He took a coverlet from the armoire and placed it over him. How would this all end? If only he would return to Mountain Grove. If only…

He walked back to his apartment feeling that with each step he lifted a hundred pounds.

Vienna in the twenties for Kirov was a place of great cultural stimulation relieving him at times from his turmoil, and he reveled in it as he had years back. He spent a great deal of his time at Cafe Llandtmann where he sat for hours sipping black coffee and, knowing it was a favorite place of Freud, hoping he might encounter him. He spent his time with architect Otto Wagner, who was making quite a name for himself, along with Ludwig Wittgenstein, a philosopher, Stefan Zweig, an author friend, Arthur Schnitzler, a play-wright, and Gustav Klimt, a painter whose gold-flecked paintings were nothing short of masterpieces to Kirov's way of thinking. Love and admiration for the arts were the center of Vienna's identity.

Intellectuals interested in psychoanalysis and being mentored stimulated his thinking and seemed entirely dis-tinct from most Viennese society. Creative thinking seemed to fill a sense of alienation; artists were motivated by creativ-ity and a passion for recognition, a potent combination.

Kirov felt he existed in heaven these times and he sensed Freud, whether present or not, forged the greatest influence. His theories of the unconscious were obviously present in his friend Zweig's writing, as well as Schnitzler's, who wrote of sexual exploitation and personal trauma.

Kirov knew someday Freud's influence would be even greater felt in America and when he returned would continue to work towards that goal. Here he felt a sense of homecom-ing. Vienna was where he had studied for years, where he had met Anna, where his family, now dead, had lived with him through so many boyhood memories. Yet, it soon turned his mind into a state of turmoil. After the long sea voyage, Freud could not see him. All he could find out was he was suffering from cancer of his mouth. He was taking no patients except, it was rumored, Marie Bonaparte, whose resistance allegedly wore him down.

He soon left for his appointment with Dr. Neuhauer. He walked the same path he so often had with Anna. And what had he done? Taken her life as she knew it away from her—her home, country, parents, all she held dear. Why hadn't he been more understanding, more observant of her moods, her hardly eating? And then the child, his greatest joy which made this alien country bearable for her. Why did he have to die? He was a doctor and should have noticed the signs sooner but was so caught up in establishing a practice to build their life together it was too late. She became insane soon after the child died. Then her parents, and he did too in a complex sort of way as he watched her disintegrate and he could do nothing. Nothing.

Then Eleanor entered the picture. And what of her? Why did she fall in love with him when she knew he was unavailable by all the signs he showed? Yet, soon he was madly in love with her. Yet, she chose other men who were equally unattainable, this Dante Ravelli, for instance? Was it a result of her fear of a real relationship? He noticed the terrified look in her eyes before they had sex. Why? What were the events in her life that caused such horrible depressions in her she often practically became immobile when they occurred?. He prayed she was working with Brodsky to help clear these things up, to free her mind as he was working with Neuhauer.

He suddenly realized he was in such deep thought he had reached Neuhauer's building. He trudged up the stairs and knocked on the door, hope in his heart.

Kirov was pleased with his progress with Neuhauer. He needed clarification for his reactions, his guilt over Anna, his love for Eleanor, working hard to overcome the demons that haunted him over his guilt concerning Anna and her death and his falling in love with Eleanor. Neuhauer helped him gain that elucidation. After many sessions, they no longer needed to meet as patient and psychoanalst and instead became good friends.

The Cafe Viennese was crowded that evening but Neuhauer's status earned them a table quickly.

They ordered bourbons, shared a wonderful meal of veal, potatoes, string beans and pastry, along with a night cap of sherry.

"Tell me, Kirov, do you really feel ready to return?"

"I do. With some reservation, I must admit."

"Of course," Neuhauer smiled. "That would be normal, I think." He took a sip of his sherry. "Time must do its job. And, truthfully, it never will completely. It is how you handle what happened, accept it, that will give you a chance at happiness. How you seize each day and make the most of it."

"I understand. We've discussed this."

"To discuss is one thing. To act upon what we have discussed. That will be your challenge."

They ate silently a time.

"Tell me more about this woman, Eleanor."

"I've told you as much as I can. She is somewhat of an enigma to me. She can be very happy one minute and in despair the next. In time, I hope she will trust working with Brodsky and she will eventually trust to tell me freely what has caused her to be so traumatized. I know surely some events in her childhood she has either repressed or will not discuss as openly as she should with me at this point. I know, as we've discussed, I must continue to gain her trust."

"In time. Brodsky is an excellent psychoanalyst. And perhaps you can fulfill her to the point of overcoming it. Live in the moment. That is all we have. Look at poor Freud. Such a brilliant mind. So much ahead of him to contribute to the world. And he develops cancer, which the rumors say is terminal."

"I had no idea it was that serious."

"They had to cut a hole in his palate to remove the cancer. He has it plugged up. Can you imagine? And, of course, being a Jew does not help with the climate some feel is beginning to emerge here."

"I refuse to believe that. We are civilized, for God's sake."

"You know what Freud would say about that."

"But we must have hope…"

"And when do you return?"

"One week. And I am still hoping for a meeting with Freud. He changed my life."

"I would not count on it."

A mood of somberness took over. So much suddenly seemed to be changing, worsening in Vienna. Yet, this mood verified Kirov's desire to return to Eleanor, to claim her as his own, let the chips fall where they may.

He tried to enjoy his last week in Vienna, saying goodbye to old friends and visiting his usual haunt, the Cafe Landtmann, still hoping to see Freud one day, visiting the Museum Belvedere Palace, its galleries. He said goodbye to his friends. He knew how much he would miss the intellectual stimulation of their conversations.

The next week he stood on the deck of the ship returning him home, staring at the ocean.

His weeks in Vienna refreshed and revived him. Only one dilemma had not been solved, the one he had run from.

And that was the agony of his love, still as strong as ever, even more so in her absence, of Eleanor.

What had happened while he was gone?

Had she chosen Charles over him?

When Kirov returned to Paterson, his apartment seemed to have a surreal quality to it. After so much time in Vienna, could he readjust, face Eleanor and her decision?

He saw Colin on the street a few days later.

They shook hands heartily enough.

"Shall we have a cup of coffee? I'll fill you in on my trip. It was very interesting."

"I—don't think so. Busy day."

Had he seen a slight look of reproach on Colin's face or imagined it? He appeared friendly enough at first glance and was uncertain how to take his friend's attitude.

At least he would surely tell Eleanor he was back, that he had seen him. That was what truly mattered, that she know he returned to her. He continued with his official duties at St. Joseph's and was filled with trepidation when he entered the Women's Alliance a few days later. He had no idea how Eleanor would greet him and now feared Colin had told her he was back and she decided their relationship was over since he had not heard from her.

"What…?" Eleanor had a startled look on her face.

"As you see, I've returned. I saw Colin a few days ago and thought he would surely tell you he had seen me. Did he?" His heart pumped hard as he spoke to her.

"No. He didn't. Or I would have come to you." She blushed. "You surely know that by now. But I have no right to say that after what you've been through. No right at all."

"I went to Vienna to get perspective. I did not see Freud but a wonderful analyst, Fritz Neuhauer, who has helped me immensely."

"I'm glad of it. And you must know Dr. Brodsky has helped me understand myself beyond belief. Still, we have to constantly continue to work on my problems. He has given me such insight."

"I fear you're angry with me for leaving as quickly as I did. Running away, really."

"Of course not. You needed time to think."

"I'm so glad you're working with Dr. Brodsky."

"Your advice to see him has helped me more than I can say."

"I still fear you're angry with me for leaving as quickly as I did."

"Of course not. Well, I was at first. But so briefly. After what happened, I understand completely."

She did not speak of the hours of sleep she lost, her deep depression, her vanished weight from her difficulty in eating after he left. Until Brodsky.

"I want to see you. Whenever you like. I want to look to the future, not think of the past. Do you feel the same?"

"I'm always there to help you, Aaron."

"That's not an answer. Perhaps this Saturday we can meet in Hawthorne. Is that possible?"

"I'll make it possible."

"Saturday then. I must examine a few patients on this listing they gave me at St. Joseph's. Will you lead me to them? And any others you'd like me to examine."

"Of course."

They were businesslike again. She led him to the patients.

One thought clanged through his mind. Why hadn't Colin told her he was back?

When Eleanor arrived home, Lily, as usual, met her at the door yelping with glee. She bent down, lifted the puppy, and snuggled her to her face, felt the tug at her heart she experienced every time she saw her.

Colin had been invited for dinner, as usual. He came to her in the kitchen. He smiled. "I got so hungry I started some potatoes in the oven."

"Good. I'll make something easy. Maybe melted cheese sandwiches with bacon? And the potatoes?"

"Sounds wonderful to me."

"You'll never guess who's back." She tried to sound casual. "Aaron Kirov. Did you know that?"

"I did."

"And why didn't you tell me? I was shocked when he appeared at the Alliance."

"And were you glad of it?"

"He's an excellent doctor. Of course I am."

"Is that all? Or is this none of your father's business?"

She grasped the back of a kitchen chair. "I don't know what to do."

"Charles is a good man. He'd move heaven and earth for you. Even go back to the hospital."

"Charles doesn't know how I feel about Aaron. And I mean to keep it that way. I wouldn't hurt him for the world."

Colin groaned inwardly. Charles had not known that day a while back when they spoke, and he thought he did. He knew now he told Charles without realizing it. Now what, dear God?

"I won't leave Charles if that's what you think. He's been too good and kind to me. I want to help him all I can. But I love Kirov and always will." Her face became etched with sorrow. "It's hopeless, I know. Hopeless."

"If it has to become a secret affair, I'd rather have that than see Charles with a broken heart. And who am I to talk of you and Aaron being in love and together? Look at me, and your mother. It happens."

She went to the ice box, turned on the radio playing "You Are Love," from *Show Boat*, one of her favorites. "Let me start dinner."

"You know, I did want to talk to you about another thing on my mind."

"Of course."

"It's—Ireland. I think I want to go back. To live. Of what use have I been here? I don't want to leave Flanagan's but am I ever goin' to make better profit commission weaving when they get back on their feet? It'll be ages before my loom's paid off. It's a big chunk of my earnings each week. And he won't let me do work as a loom fixer since he's got a man. And then, there's my thoughts of Ireland. Michael Collins. I think of him every day, what happened to him. I still even dream of him. Then there's Paddy who I miss dearly. I guess I miss Ireland more than I thought I would."

"And what about me? I need you. I can't cope with Charles on my own. You'd go so easily?"

"I didn't say I was sure, did I? But—"

She burst into tears. "You're my father!" She realized now if Colin had not told her about seeing Kirov returned it was a definite sign he favored Charles. Was this the bargaining chip that would make him stay in New Jersey? That would force her to give up Kirov?

"You need to choose. Or it will destroy you in the end. In truth, I do think Charles knows. Men sense such things." He did not have the courage to tell her he inadvertently told him.

How could she survive this? She and Charles had not had sex in such a time. He had become impotent from the alcohol. And that now caused her greatest fear, and joy.

She was carrying Kirov's child.

The one happiness Charles had was the miraculous device rather recently developed, the radio. That morning he was sitting on the sofa, absorbed in a radio interview with Charles Lindbergh who was planning to fly across Atlantic Ocean and land at Le Bourget Airfield in Paris to complete his crossing.

"Good heavens, I can hardly believe it. Admiral Richard Byrd flying to the North Pole and now Lindbergh—

Eleanor stood above him.

She was finally ready to follow one aspect of Dr. Brodsky's advice.

"Charles, we have to talk."

He rubbed his eyes.

"Can't I just listen to this interview with Charles Lindberg first?"

"This is more important. Will you go back to the hospital for help?"

He turned the radio off.

"May I ask you a question?"

"Of course."

"Why in God's name have you stayed with me?" He ran his fingers through his hair. "I can't beat this. I just can't."

"I don't believe that. People have done it, but it takes great strength. I believe in you. You're stronger than you think."

"I don't know that I am."

"Of course you are."

"Do you really think so?"

Just then Lily ran into the room, yelping and scratching at Eleanor's shoes. She lifted the dog in her arms, cuddled her, thought of this last act of kindness of Charles, amidst so many, during the bleak moments of her life.

And it was in that moment she made her decision and vowed not to change her mind.

She would give up Kirov and stay with Charles under one condition.

"If you promise to go back to the hospital, I'll stay with you. You can't do this alone. We can rebuild our lives again. Of course we can."

They did not speak for a time, each lost in thought.

"All right. I'll go," he finally said, defeat written across his face.

He embraced her.

She could sense he was crying.

She would keep her vow at all costs. Charles' dependable love was always there for her and she would reciprocate.

She would give up Kirov, although she knew she would always love him. But the child she carried. What to do about the child?

Kirov was reading a study in hysteria when he heard the light knocking on the door, which he knew was Eleanor.

When he opened it, he was taken aback. She had been crying, dark circles lay beneath her eyes, and she was trembling.

"You look terrible. I'll make you a hot toddy. How I've thought of you all day and felt the hours were moving so slowly. And now you're here and I feel such peace." He encircled his arms around her and held her gently. "Though I'm worried you don't look well and something's troubling you." He turned to his medical bag. "Let me take your vital signs. I hope you're not coming down with something."

"It—isn't that."

"Just sit and rest until after you have your drink."

It calmed her down. She was grateful for the toddy which would help her say some of the most difficult words she had ever spoken.

"Charles is doing terribly, I'm afraid."

"Have you mentioned hospitalization again?"

"He—needs more than medical help."

Kirov's face turned ashen.

"He needs me, fully, completely. I think I've known it such a long time, but my love for you blinds me. I've looked away. Not wanting to face the agony because of the love I feel for you." She clenched her hands around the cup. "Which I'll feel for you until the day I die. But I can't live two lives any longer. I can't. It's tearing me apart. I must devote my full self to Charles. I've decided, as Dr. Brodsky said I must, that only I can accomplish this."

Still he did not speak.

"It's hopeless, Aaron. We both know that. In our deepest hearts. You're—free now. God knows, because of the most tragic circumstances, which nearly destroyed you not only because of the way Anna died but with the knowledge you were unfaithful to her. Though you have not spoken of it. Don't you think I realize that's why you left for Vienna, to sort things out with this Dr. Neuhauer, and work on the guilt you felt?"

"It was very—complicated" was all he could offer.

She sat on the nearest chair, clenched her hands around the cup. "And now I'm in a similar situation. Just as difficult. Charles has seen me at my worst, loved me unconditionally throughout our marriage."

"Don't you think I would feel the same way?"

"Of course. But he's so fragile. And what we experienced together, so much, the worst being the death of our child."

She began to tremble. He pulled up a chair, sat next to her, held her hand in his.

"Finally quite a while after our marriage and Charles' patience with my sexual fears, I told him about being abused as a little girl. I thought he would denounce me as—unclean. Instead, he accepted me and said he loved me unconditionally."

"Don't you think I would feel the same way?"

"Of course. But he's so fragile. Not as strong as you."

"I have thought about this constantly. Your dark moods. If we are together, I can help you overcome them. I know I can help you if you slip back."

"Do you think so? I don't know anymore. But all I do know is that I have to be there completely for him or I can no longer live with myself."

She saw sorrow etched upon his face, a look she would remember the rest of her life.

"I've made my choice. I can't live this way and I can't desert Charles. You and I are at a dead-end street. We both know it."

He swallowed hard, could not speak.

"I think you should ask for a permanent residency at St. Joseph's. It will be for the best."

"Of course." His voice was hardly audible.

He took out a pencil and paper from his desk. "I— have a new telephone number. I'll—give it to you. I only ask that you promise that if you—ever need me, you call." He scratched his number on a pad, tore it off, handed it to her. "Remember, if you ever need me—"

She wept unashamedly as she prepared to leave.

"Can we know one more embrace before you go? One that must last a lifetime?"

She wiped her tears from her face. "I can't understand why you would still want me. I'm so—flawed. But Dr. Brodsky sees great hope for me and with his help I'm beginning to see I must make important choices. If I take you in my arms, I fear I'll change my mind on everything I've said. I don't know how I'll endure without you. But I've made my decision. And I'll honor it."

"My dear, we are all flawed. We just have to keep trying to be better. And honor. If only we did not believe in honor."

She walked to the door, turned to study one last time the man who owned her heart and soul and always would.

And then she left, along with the precious child that grew within her.

Colin realized the moment of truth had come. Ever since he thought back of the day he told Charles of Eleanor and Kirov's relationship and the reaction he had seen on Charles' face, though he tried to disguise it, he felt convinced more and more he must confess to her.

Eleanor arrived and poured herself a glass of whiskey, unusual for her. She drank some and plopped onto the sofa, the soothing liquid helping to calm her.

"Eleanor, I must tell you. Charles knows about you and Kirov."

Eleanor gulped the rest of the whiskey down, scrutinized Colin.

"What are you saying?"

"I told him by mistake, fool that I am. I thought he knew, and I said you and Kirov were in love. That it would surely pass. If Charles got help. As soon as I mentioned your relationship, it was like Charles saw a ghost. He could hardly speak."

"When did you tell him?"

"Months ago at least."

"So he knew my disappearances on days on the week end wasn't because I was going to the Alliance?"

"I'm sure of it."

"Oh, God. But he never confronted me. Never."

"Maybe he thought it would burn itself out. I don't know."

She felt little pain at this point. The whiskey did its job well. She stumbled toward the stairs. "I just want to sleep right now. I'll cope with this tomorrow. I just can't right now."

"I understand. I feel terrible about it. But I didn't realize—"

"It's not your fault. He would have found out sooner or later. Please, I need to get to bed."

He watched the woman who had so often shown such courage and strength slumped and slowly walking up the stairs, holding onto the banister for dear life. In that moment, he knew he would stay with her and never leave her for Ireland.

The next morning she woke up with a headache that sapped all her energy. What a fool she had been to drink that horrible whiskey. She decided a walk in the cool air of the coming day would refresh her. The seasons never ceased to be a miracle to Eleanor. What she admired most was their reliability in a world that often let her down. One could tolerate winter because surely spring would eventually arrive. The leaves brushed her shoes as she walked. She could see the sedum showing the last vestige of autumn, clinging to life. The vines that curled the fences around the area of her property still glowed in gold and red splendor.

She decided to walk to the mill district, drawn as always by her past, observed the First Ward Library where her mother used to take her when she learned how to read and discovered new worlds outside of the tenement. And Paterson's Great

Falls, still flowing on eternally. She studied the flood-damaged buildings slowly being restored. Would Paterson survive and return to its former glory? A residue of loss permeated her to the bone, a dark chasm of inconsolable sorrow, her sadness filling her with fear, a Paterson that would eventually become a mere shadow of what it had been when she was a little girl. She sat on the bench near the Falls, covered her face and wept.

The next day Charles emerged at the top of the stairs, suitcase in hand. How different he looked from the robust man she first met and thought was the gardener at Lafferty's estate. He stood slumped, his eyes etched with red veins, as were his cheeks, his face flushed. How much was her fault? If she had never met him might he have been saved? But he had fallen in love with her and was his fate sealed? She must live with that knowledge the rest of her life and must continue to work with Dr. Brodsky. An unspeakable sadness swept over her. Then she remembered what he had told her. Not guilt, but regret. Why couldn't she have loved him as deeply as he loved her?

She plopped onto the nearest chair. Her beloved Paterson endangered, her loss of Kirov. And Charles. Would he recover? Yet, she would keep her word and stand by him. At all costs. Brodsky had given her more ability to cope with all her demons than she thought imaginable.

"You're packed already? Isn't it the end of the week you're going to Mountain Grove?"

"I'm not packed to go back there. I'm leaving you, Eleanor. For good."

"What—?"

She felt enmeshed in a net of confusion.

"I'm leaving you."

"But why?"

"Because you deserve a chance at happiness. With Kirov who can also continue to help you. Because you deserve better than me."

She attempted to rise, finally did, and moved towards him with all the strength she could muster.

"I couldn't find a man kinder than you've been to me. You must believe me."

"I do. But kindness is one thing. Love is another. I'm not the man you deserve. If I went back to the hospital, I'd get dried out, no doubt. But after I'd come home a time, I'd be drinking again. And possibly hurting you." He covered his face. "Good God, that I did that!"

He faced her squarely then. "In my deepest heart, you see, I don't want to give up drinking. I can't. It's my best companion. My comfort." He half smiled. "Like the dearest of friends. It gets me through the day. It's as simple as that."

"Charles, I want you to know. About Robbie. It's taken me a long time to say it but—with all my heart, I forgive you. I truly do for taking him to the mill. I realize now more than I ever did before you never dreamed how dangerous it could be. Dr. Brodsky and I have talked of this a great deal."

He clasped her hand.

"You can't imagine what it means to me to hear you say that."

"But if you don't get help, it will destroy you in the end." Her eyes misted. "Don't you want us to have a life together? We could have a good life if only you'd—"

"I know I can't beat it, you see. And the main point is I don't want to. I live for that drink, especially the one that will take me to oblivion. I know I can't live without it now."

"But you can get help! I know it. Maybe psychiatry. Why can't you try it?"

"With Kirov, I suppose."

She blushed.

"Of course not. Perhaps Dr. Brodsky. He's a wonderful doctor."

"No, I don't think so. You know, I have nothing but good will towards Kirov if he can finally give you the happiness you deserve. I mean it. You've been through hell—the abuse, the near starvation from the strike, the murder of your mother, my flaws, Robbie's—I don't have to go on. The point is this. I want your happiness. And I can't give it to you. And I don't want you stuck with an alcoholic who'll always be a ball and chain around your neck."

He also knew from his readings by Freud it's not uncommon for a neurosis to return after major traumatic events, but he did not mention it. He realized Kirov could help her if she did begin to fail again.

"I've never felt you were—"

"Now, don't deny what I've put you through. I want to do this Eleanor. For you." He paused. "And your child."

Her heart splintered.

"You know?"

"Of course I do. I'm not that lacking in observation. And the child. That's another reason I'm leaving. You're everything to me and I want to give you and the child the gift of my leaving to prove it. I know you love Kirov and he can finally give you happiness. I'm certain of it. I never can. And I want to free you to know that happiness. That's all I ask. That will be my greatest joy."

She began to weep, could hardly speak. "I'm—so—sorry, Charles. For all of it."

"Sorry? Why? You'll have a son or daughter. And Kirov will be a wonderful father. I'll be at the Bellevue a few days or so to get things moving along with my lawyer for a divorce. I'll have him call you. The house, whatever you want, is yours. I just need enough to get by, find a place to live. And you know I made a good profit from the mills. Plus there's the money my father left me. We'll figure it all out with the lawyer. As for me, I'm not sure where I'll wind up. Perhaps the Carolinas. I've been reading a lot about them lately. The articles say they're beautiful. Certainly far from Paterson. Too many memories wherever I look."

She began to tremble, squeezed her arms across her chest.

"This isn't happening. It can't be."

"But it is. It's for the best. You know that deep inside yourself."

"Charles—"

"I love you so much." He embraced her.

"Now, now. No more tears. You call Kirov as soon as you can. I have one request. When you think of me, keep a remembrance of the good times. When we first met. The carousel. When you see the garden in bloom, think of me. Only the joy we knew. Not the sorrow. I would be so glad if you do that. Do you promise? Promise to remember the good times?

"I—promise."

"Goodbye, my dear." He swallowed hard. "I can't give you much, but I can give you a chance at happiness. I truly believe you will find that with Kirov. And your child. I don't expect to see you again. After the lawyer straightens things out."

"But not knowing where you are, how you are—"

And could she pick up the shreds of what was left of her and start a new life?

She held him tighter in her arms one last time, touched the face she would never see again, caressed it, stricken by loss. She would keep her promise. She would remember him every day, for memory is stronger than death and the heart is as wide as the world.

He brushed the tears from her face, only to find more reappear. After a time he released her, picked up his suitcase, walked to the door, opened it, did not turn, then closed it.

He was gone.

She watched him from the window, walking down the long path, past the twining mandevilla, reaching towards heaven, the caladium, sedum, glowing gold in the sun.

Yes, she would be nourished by remembering him this way, in the garden.

Soon he disappeared in the distance. Yes, she would wonder about him every day of her life, for nothing loved is ever lost.

She thought of their first date, the carousel; as a young girl it was the first time she remembered being truly happy. And the song playing as they swirled round and round to its music:

Meet me tonight in Dreamland,
Under the silv'ry moon;

Yet, she knew she must go forward. Her child stirred in her womb. Was it coincidence? Or destiny? But she knew one thing. This was her chance to keep working on extinguishing the past, to begin anew.

She reached into her pocket and once again felt the piece of paper she had fondled so often, the one Kirov had given her with his new phone number, crinkled from her touch.

She went to the telephone. She picked up the receiver, held it in her trembling hand a time.

She put it back upon its cradle.

She would call Kirov.

But not quite yet.

Bibliography

I owe a great debt to those writers whose books and research were so helpful and inspirational and wish to acknowledge them and their work.

Aronowitz, Robert A. Unnatural History: Breast Cancer and American Society

Barry, John. The Great Influenza: The Epic Story of the Deadliest Plague in History

Breuer, Joseph and Sigmund Freud. Studies in Hysteria

Chernow, Ronald. Titan: The Life of John D. Rockefeller

Chittick, James. Silk Manufacture and Its Problems

Corbett, Glenn. The Great Paterson Fire of 1902: The Story of New Jersey's Biggest Blaze

Crosby, Alfred. America's Forgotten Pandemic: The Influenza of 1918

Denker, Henry. A Far Country

Edelman, Bernard. Centenarians: The Story of the Twentieth Century by the Americans Who Lived It

Freud, Sigmund. The Basic Writings of Sigmund Freud

Freud, Sigmund. The Interpretation of Dreams

Golin, Steve. The Fragile Bridge: The Paterson Silk Strike:1913 Gollaher, David. Voices of the Mad: The Life of Dorothea Dix

Grob, Gerald N. The Mad Among Us: A History of the Care of America's Mentally Ill

History of Schizophrenia Treatments. Internet

History of Schizophrenia and Other Madness. Internet

Johnston, William M. Vienna: The Golden Age 1815-1914

Jones, Ernest. The Life and Works of Sigmund Freud

Kolata, Gina. Flu: The Story of the Great Influenza Epidemic
    of 1918 and the Search for the Virus That Caused It

Lehane, Dennis. Shutter Island

Mackay, James. Michael Collins

McCarthy, Katherine. Early Alcoholism Treatment: The
    Emmanuel Movement and Richard Peabody—Internet

Medscape. Historical Roots of Schizophrenia—Internet

Muckenhoupt, Margaret. Sigmund Freud: Explorer of the
    Unconscious

Okrent, Daniel. Last Call: The Rise and Fall of Prohibition

Schizophrenia Treatment. Health and Wellness article
    —Internet

Scranton, Philip., ed. Silk City, "The Battle for Labor

Supremacy in Paterson, 1916-1922," "Labor Conflict and-
    Technological Change: The Family Shop in Paterson"
    Stone, The Passions of the Mind

The American Scholar. "Vienna: Trapped in a Golden
    Age"—posted by Alexandra Starr on Internet

The Great Pandemic: 1918: State by State Internet

Tracy, Sarah W. Alcoholism in America

Wukovitz, John F. The 1920s: America's Decades